PRAISE FOR THE
DREAMHOUSE KINGS SERIES

"If you like creepy and mysterious, this is the house for you! Every room opens a door to magic, true horror, and amazing surprises. I loved wandering around in these books. With a house of so many great, haunting stories, why would you ever want to go outside?"

—R.L. STINE, BEST-SELLING AUTHOR OF THE
FEAR STREET AND GOOSEBUMPS SERIES

"To call the Dreamhouse Kings series a young adult novel is not to do this splendid tale justice. With Harry Potter sadly retired, here is a series ready to step in and fill that massive void. The same portal that spirits brothers Xander and David off on a journey through time whisks us away across a brilliant landscape of imagination and adventure. A new and future classic in the world of young adult fiction."

—JON LAND, BESTSELLING AUTHOR OF
THE SEVEN SINS: THE TYRANT ASCENDING

"Dreamhouse Kings is a non-stop action ride into history's wildest adventures. It's my new favorite series!"

—SLADE PEARCE, AGE 13, ACTOR
(*OCTOBER ROAD, AIR BUDDIES*)

timescape

BOOKS BY THIS AUTHOR

Comes a Horseman

Germ

Deadfall

Deadlock

DREAMHOUSE KINGS SERIES

1 House of Dark Shadows

2 Watcher in the Woods

3 Gatekeepers

4 Timescape

5 Whirlwind

6 Frenzy

timescape

BOOK FOUR OF
DREAMHOUSE KINGS

ROBERT LIPARULO

THOMAS NELSON
Since 1798

NASHVILLE   DALLAS   MEXICO CITY   RIO DE JANEIRO

Published in Nashville, Tennessee, by Thomas Nelson. Thomas Nelson is a registered trademark of Thomas Nelson, Inc.

Page design by Mandi Cofer
Map design by Doug Cordes

Thomas Nelson, Inc., books may be purchased in bulk for educational, business, fund-raising, or sales promotional use. For information, please e-mail SpecialMarkets@ThomasNelson.com.

Publisher's Note: This novel is a work of fiction. Names, characters, places, and incidents are either products of the author's imagination or used fictitiously. All characters are fictional, and any similarity to people living or dead is purely coincidental.

Unless otherwise noted, Scripture quotations are taken from HOLY BIBLE: NEW INTERNATIONAL VERSION®. © 1973, 1978, 1984 by International Bible Society. Used by permission of Zondervan Publishing House. All rights reserved.

ISBN 978-1-59554-893-1 (trade paper)

Library of Congress Cataloging-in-Publication Data

Liparulo, Robert.
  Timescape / Robert Liparulo.
    p. cm. — (Dreamhouse Kings ; bk. 4)
  Summary: David, Xander, Dad, and Keal discover that Taksidian wants their house for himself in order to use the time portals to build an empire, and unless they can find his weakness in time, the future of the world itself may be in danger.
  ISBN 978-1-59554-500-8 (hardcover)
  [1. Time travel—Fiction. 2. Dwellings—Fiction. 3. Supernatural—Fiction. 4. Horror stories.] I. Title.
  PZ7.L6636Tim 2009
  [Fic]—dc22

                                        2009012367

Printed in the United States of America

10 11 12 13 14 RRD 5 4 3 2 1

FOR MATTHEW

*"It is not flesh and blood,
but heart which makes us father and son."*

STOP!

READ *HOUSE OF DARK SHADOWS,*
WATCHER IN THE WOODS,
AND *GATEKEEPERS*
BEFORE CONTINUING!

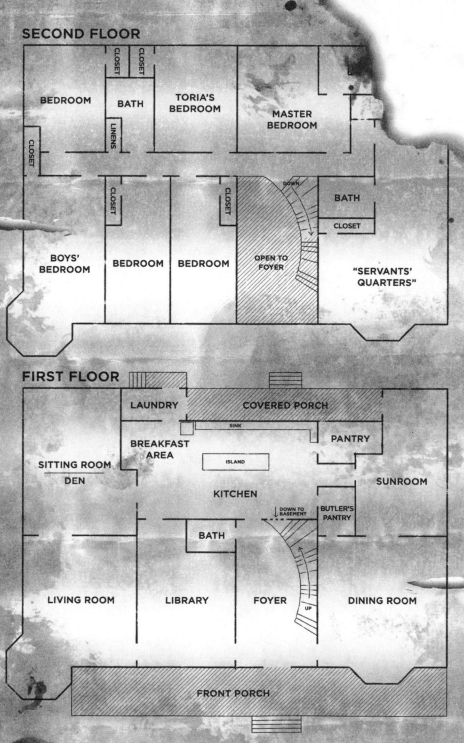

*"It's not the size of the dog in the fight,
it's the size of the fight in the dog."*
—MARK TWAIN

"Never, never, never, never give up."
—WINSTON CHURCHILL

CHAPTER

one

David watched the horde of humanlike creatures surge up the incline toward them.

"Dad?" he croaked. He reached out for his father, but Dad was too far away. His legs refused to budge, locked in place by the sight of the approaching creatures—their spindly limbs jittering up and down as they climbed, their pale skin almost glowing in the sunlight, their mouths spewing out howls and snarls, their eyes crazy, desperate.

Along with his dad and Keal, Uncle Jesse's caretaker and friend, David stood at the top of a hill between two valleys: the one behind them, peaceful and pristine; the one in front cradling the ruins of Los Angeles. Between them and the destroyed buildings lay a massive junkyard of concrete slabs, rusted hunks of automobiles, twisted and broken debris. It all seemed to have been blown against the hill, the way litter gathers in gutters. It was from this trash dump that the creatures had emerged.

And as soon as they had spotted the Kings and Keal, the creatures attacked.

Creatures, David thought. They were human—something about them told him it was true—but they were so different, so animalistic, so . . . *creature*like.

"Hey!" Xander yelled. He was thirty paces down the peaceful side of the hill. "Let's go! What are you waiting for?"

David turned, yearning to be tearing down the valley with his brother, putting acres of distance between himself and the approaching horde. He called, "Dad says the portal's that way, toward"—he glanced at the creatures, getting closer—"toward *them!*"

Dad and Keal held the items from the antechamber: a parasol, a butterfly net, a picnic basket. The stupid things had given them no clue of the dangers they had just walked into—not the way the helmet, shield, and chain mail had predicted Xander's journey to the Roman Colosseum. But the items served another purpose. Besides allowing whoever possessed them to open the portal door, the one that led from their house in present-day Pinedale, California, to some other time, some other place, they also showed the way home by tugging you to the portal that would take you back.

Right now, they were urging Dad and Keal to descend into the other valley, right into the arms of the creatures. David shook his head: everything about this world was messed up.

"What?" Xander said. His mouth hung open, only slightly wider than his eyes. Fear made him appear much younger than his fifteen years. He waved at the woods and meadow below him. "But we came from over there!"

David knew Xander understood the portals better than that. The portals' homes *sometimes* appeared near the ones that dropped them into the other worlds, but they could be anywhere.

"Not this time, Xander!" he said.

But that didn't matter, did it? They couldn't follow the items' prodding, not now. He broke from his stance and crashed into his father. He pushed him toward Xander. "Dad, let's go— anywhere but down there!"

Dad nodded. He hooked a hand around the cast on David's broken left arm and pulled David away from the creatures. The one nearest was so close David could hear its panting and the rattling of the pebbles it dislodged as it scrambled up the hill; he could see a thread of spit spilling over its trembling bottom lip.

Keal rushed forward, pistol in hand. He thumbed the hammer back.

David tore away from his father's grasp. "No!" he yelled. He stretched out his left arm. His cast prevented him from reaching Keal's arm, but then he lunged with his right, catching Keal's bicep, knocking his aim toward the sky. David squeezed his eyes closed, expecting the sharp crack of the firearm. When it didn't come, he looked: Keal was glaring down at him.

"David!" he said.

But the creature had stopped mere feet from the top of the hill, almost on top of them. He stared at David, blinking, confused or startled. An old scar ran vertically down his face from forehead to jaw. There seemed to be no muscle separating his facial bones from the white skin that clung to them: sharp cheek bones and chin; hollow cheeks, and eyes almost lost in the pits of his sockets. His head seemed too large for his scrawny neck and bony body. Wispy brown hair clung to his skull and sprouted here and there on his face.

Keal pushed David away. He skipped closer to the creature, brought his foot up, and kicked the thing in the chest.

The creature flew backward, arms flailing. He crashed into another of his kind, and they both tumbled down the hill. Dust billowed in their wake. Other creatures moved out of their way. One leaped over them, caught his foot, and went down. He was back up in a flash, scowling. He lowered himself and scampered toward them on all fours. Dozens more around him scurried up the hill.

Keal pointed the pistol at the clouds and squeezed the trigger.

Instinctively, David ducked. The sound was loud and sharp, thunder from a lightning bolt in his ears.

The creatures must have thought so too. They all stopped. Several fell back, tumbled, turned, tried to get their feet under them as they moved down the hill toward the rubble below. Others backed away more slowly. One howled, and the others joined in. Their voices grew in volume, a chorus of angry, scared screams. To David, it was somehow worse, more piercing than the gunshot. He covered his ears.

Keal fired at the clouds again.

The howling voices spiked even louder. More creatures turned and ran.

Some held their ground. One, then another, and another, began climbing again.

David felt a tug on his collar. Dad was pulling at him. Without a word, Keal wrapped a powerful arm around David's waist, picked him up, and began jogging down the opposite incline. Dad fell in beside them. Xander saw them coming. He spun and booked toward the valley in long, pinwheeling strides.

Every time Keal's foot hit the ground, David felt his ribs crush between the man's body and arm. Air pumped out of his lungs like a bellows. More painful was the damage to his pride: he was twelve, and Keal was carrying him like a baby.

"Put . . . me . . . *down!*" he said, each word pushed out on a gust of breath. "Keal!"

Keal didn't slow, but he did turn David's feet toward the ground. When David's kicking matched Keal's pace, the big man let him go. David stumbled forward, stayed up, and darted ahead. The woods at the bottom of the hill were still a long way off. Ahead of him, Xander lurched forward, then his feet slid out from under him. He fell back, bounced off the ground, and was back up and running faster than David would have thought possible.

David looked behind him. The first of the pursuing creatures appeared on the crest of the hill, and started down toward them.

CHAPTER

two

Flat on her stomach, Nana slid backward up the third-floor stairs toward the hallway of doors.

Toria crouched on her grandmother's back, holding on with everything she had—a grotesque horsey ride in which neither horse nor rider had any fun. Nana grabbed at every step.

"Hold on, Nana!" Toria screamed.

7

But Nana's fingers would slip off one step, then another, and the two of them would bang up, up, up.

"No!" Toria yelled. She swung her head around, expecting to see someone, something at the top, waiting for them. No one was there, just the light from the hallway, flickering on and off. She knew what was happening. Jesse—her great-great-great uncle, or something like that—had talked about it the night before: the portals wanted Nana back. *Time* wanted her back, and it was pulling her back. But she belonged here. After thirty years, she had made it home. It wasn't fair! It wasn't fair!

"Let go, Toria!" Nana yelled. "You have to—" Her fingers slipped.

They bounded up three more steps. Almost to the top.

Nana groaned. "You have to stay here, Toria. You can't let it take you too!"

Toria gripped tighter. She knew her weight must have been awful for Nana, pushing her into the stairs, as the force yanked them up. She didn't care. She wasn't going to let her grandmother go.

"Jesse!" Toria called toward the hallway at the bottom of the stairs.

The big men who had come out of the portals earlier that day had broken down the two walls that separated this staircase from the main house. Now it was a straight shot to the second floor. But Jesse was hidden around a corner. He had come to help when the pull on Nana had started. He had grabbed Nana's wrists, but lost his grip. Now he was down there somewhere, crawling without his wheelchair.

"*Jesse!*"

Nana let out a painful-sounding grunt, and they shot up the rest of the stairs and jarred to a stop. Toria almost flipped off her grandmother's back. She caught herself, clutching her hands on Nana's shoulders. Nana was holding on to the sides of the doorway. Her legs hovered a few inches off the floor, quivering under the strain of the pull.

"Hold on, Nana," Toria said. She pushed her face into the fabric between the woman's shoulder blades. "Hold on," she whispered. "Please hold on."

CHAPTER

three

"Wait! Wait!"

Keal stopped them before they'd reached the woods. Xander was the farthest down. He skidded and wound up on his backside again. He got up, brushing away dirt and grass.

David stopped more slowly. When he turned, Keal was facing uphill. The creatures had reversed direction and were heading away, back over the crest. As they walked, their oversized heads swiveled to cast curious glances over their shoulders. Again one howled, and the others joined in. Only one remained facing Keal, Dad, David, and Xander. He was braced on the hill, bony shoulders rising and falling. He yelled an unintelligible word and clawed at the air toward them. He gestured to his comrades, urging them to continue the attack, then screamed in what David thought was frustration when they ignored him.

"They weren't after us," David whispered. "They just wanted us gone, away from their home."

The creature seemed to stare right at David for a long time. David wondered what he—and Xander, Dad, and Keal—would do if the guy suddenly ran for them. That made him think of the gun, and he saw that Keal had returned it to his waistband. The back of his shirt was hiked up over it.

David touched Dad's arm. He said, "Let's go. Keal, come on."

Keal held up an open hand.

The lone creature finally turned and trudged back up the hill. At the top, he looked at them once more, then disappeared down the other side.

Dad rubbed David's shoulder. He said, "What are you thinking, Keal?"

"I'm thinking we gotta get to that portal."

He turned, and David saw in his face the Army Ranger Keal used to be.

Keal said, "Right, Ed?"

Dad nodded.

Keal held up the tam-o'-shanter and blanket Xander had given him in the antechamber. "And these things say it's over that hill."

Dad hefted the butterfly net and looked at the picnic basket that was lifting off his body, tethered to his neck by a strap. "That's right."

"If those creatures are guarding that area," Keal said, "we're not going to get to it . . . *easily*."

"It moves," Xander said, stepping up to David's side. "The portal moves. It drifts around."

"You want to *wait* for it?" Keal said.

David looked into Dad's and Xander's faces. None of them wanted to wait. David wasn't even sure they could; they'd always assumed the time they could spend in the other worlds was limited. And the items became more insistent about getting home the longer they stayed. He didn't want to think what would happen if the items started *dragging* them, kicking and screaming, into those creatures' camp.

"Didn't think so," Keal said. "Look, from what you've told me, these items will lead us right to the portal. I say, let's make a run for it."

"What?" Xander said. "Through those . . . *things*, those creatures that just came after us?"

Keal shrugged. "They're scrawny."

David wished he felt Keal's confidence.

"Come on," Keal prompted. He took a step up the hill, stopped to wait for them.

Dad's brows came together. He looked into each of his sons' eyes. He said, "Stay close."

"But, Dad . . ." Xander started. His lips closed on his words. He shook his head and started to climb.

four

WEDNESDAY, 6:36 P.M.

The flickering lights cranked up the dial on Toria's panic. They fluttered on and off quickly, almost in time with her heartbeat. She lifted her head off Nana's back to look along the crooked hallway. Way down, toward the farthest wall, a steady bright glow splashed against the floor, wall, and ceiling. It must have been coming from an open portal door. That meant the door to the antechamber leading to the portal was also open. The force tugging on Nana must be coming from there.

A wind blew past, brushing the hair off her face. She couldn't feel the pull, but she felt the wind. Chilly, like the air when the family went to Mammoth Mountain for skiing lessons.

"Hold on, Nana," she said again, and slid onto the floor. She rose and ran for the light.

"Toria!" Nana called. "What're you doing? Don't go near it!"

"The door, Nana!" she yelled. "I'm going to shut it!"

I am. I am. I'm going to shut it.

The flickering light came from lamps mounted to the walls between the doors—creepy things carved to look like fighting warriors or faces or animals. Their strobing—darkness, light, darkness, light—made Toria feel like she was moving through the hallway in jittery jumps, leaping forward, then stopping, leaping again. She concentrated on the steady glow at the end of the hall and kept running.

As she approached, the air grew colder. Her tears felt icy. A light spray of water stung her cheeks.

Then she was there, squinting into the light that poured from the open portal door and filled the antechamber. Water droplets blew in with the light, swirled around the room. The wooden floor glistened with wetness. It smelled salty, like the ocean. She started to take a step into the small room, but immediately she felt her feet sucked out from under her. She fell, twisted, grabbed the edge of the door frame, just as Nana was doing at the other end of the hall.

Now Toria *did* feel the pull. It gripped her like hands, tugging her toward the portal. It was as if the portal didn't care who was in the antechamber—it wanted someone. An image flashed through her mind: the antechamber was a mouth, the portal was the throat. She remembered what Jesse had said about the house: *it's hungry.*

The wind wailed in her ears. Her hair whipped around, slapping her face.

She pulled and kicked, her sock feet slipping against the slick floor. She hooked her elbow against the hallway side of the wall and rolled until she was completely free from the pull. Then she sat, leaning her back against the wall. She breathed—panted.

"Toria!" Nana yelled.

"I'm okay." Toria stood and tried to grab the handle of the antechamber door. Invisible hands pulled at her hand, her arm. She couldn't reach the handle, and she couldn't risk leaning in any farther. Probably the door would not remain shut anyway. It would open again, lips parting for a bite.

As she ran toward her grandmother, the flickering engulfed her again. "Keep holding on, Nana."

"Can't . . ." Nana said. Her legs fluttered, as though she were clinging to the wing of an airplane instead of a door frame.

Toria grabbed one end of the ladder her brother Xander had used to mount the camera above the doorway to the landing. It was heavy and awkward, but she managed to drag it back to the antechamber. She laid it lengthwise on the floor across the opening. It was something, anyway.

She returned to Nana. She knelt at her feet, pushed the bottoms of them. They wobbled under her palms, as though she were trying to connect two magnets.

Crack!

Nana's feet shoved Toria back six inches. A piece of the door frame had snapped away. Nana was holding it, uselessly. Her other hand gripped the opposite side of the opening. Nana released the length of wood, stretched, and reclaimed a grip on the edge.

Toria shifted over her grandmother to the landing. She clutched both hands on Nana's wrist, put her feet against the wall, and pulled.

"I got you," Toria said. "But don't let go." Movement at the bottom of the stairs caught her eye. "Jesse! Je—"

Not Jesse.

Taksidian stood staring up at her. The man who wanted them out of the house, who had chased David, who had gotten the town to try to evict them. Cloaked in shadows, his face caught the flickering light, flashing like a skull in a haunted house. Toria screamed.

Taksidian shook his head, the strobing light making it look like he was snapping his face back and forth. "I got *you*," he said, mocking Toria's words to her grandmother.

His shoe clicked down the first step, and he rose toward her.

CHAPTER

five

"Doesn't look so bad," David whispered.

"If you think sticking your head in a garbage disposal isn't bad," Xander said.

Crawling on their bellies, they had just reached the top of the hill. Below them, the creatures were mingling around the boulder-sized clumps of concrete, wrecked cars, and other refuse. Many were squatting down in small groups, as though discussing something. Earlier, when the creatures had come after them, David had not recognized any words, but he guessed they must have some way to communicate, some sort of language.

"Looks like a lot of them are leaving," he pointed out. Scores of them were picking their way through the rough terrain of trash toward the ruins of the city.

"Probably heading out to forage for food," Dad said.

Keal slid backward, away from the crest. David, Dad, and Xander followed. When they were far enough down the hill to kneel without being seen, they huddled together.

"Why would Jesse send us here?" Xander asked Dad through clenched teethed. "To such a dangerous place?"

"He didn't send 'us,'" Dad reminded him. "You and David followed Keal and me on your own."

David could tell his brother was trying not to look guilty.

Dad continued: "Besides, he was trying to explain what we'd find here when Keal fell through the portal."

Xander waved his hand over his head. "But this has nothing to do with *finding Mom.*"

Their mother had been kidnapped into one of the worlds, and ever since then their lives had been consumed by trying to rescue her.

"Jesse wanted us to see the destroyed city, the future," David said glumly. "To know how bad it gets . . . if we don't stop it."

"Stop it?" Xander said. "How?"

"Worry about that later," Keal said, glancing up toward the ridge. "We gotta get out of here." He looked at each of them. "Ready?"

"No," Xander snapped.

Dad gripped Xander's shoulder and spoke to Keal. "You go first. Keep your cap and blanket in front of you. Follow their pull. David, you grab Keal's belt. Don't let go. Xander, hold on to your brother's belt. I'll bring up the rear."

Keal reached behind him and produced the pistol.

"Don't—" David said.

"Just to scare them," Keal said. He read the concern on David's face. "I promise."

"Unless you *have* to," Xander said. "Right? You'll use it on them if you have to?"

Keal said nothing, and David didn't know what to say: *have to* was *have to*.

Dad said, "If you can't feel the pull, or my things tug me in a different direction, I'll take the lead. Deal?"

"Let's do it," Keal said. He stood.

David slipped his fingers around Keal's belt and felt Xander grab his. He leaned closer to his brother and whispered, "Strong and courageous."

Xander smiled—the first smile David had seen in a while.

Keal bolted forward, nearly yanking David off his feet. He fell in step, and they went over the hill. They were twenty paces down when the first of the creatures spotted them. It stood, pointed, started howling.

A bloodcurdling scream—close—seemed to knock David's heart out of his chest. Then he realized it was Keal. The man was howling back at the creatures, making the scariest lion roars David had ever heard come out of a human. Maybe it was to psych himself up for the plunge into enemy territory or to scare the tar out of the creatures, but whatever the reason, David liked it. He began screaming himself, an airy, high-pitched squeak at first, then deep, loud, get-out-of-my-way yells. Behind him, Xander's and Dad's voices kicked in. They were a freight train of hurt steaming down the hill.

The creatures scattered, disappearing into the rubble or hurling their bodies over it, tumbling to get away. But not all of them: a dozen or more actually stepped forward. Watching the four of them coming, these drew together. They began picking up rocks.

Keal stopped screaming long enough to say, "Watch your step!"

They hit the first of the rubble, chunks of concrete the size of watermelons. David jumped over them, on them, swerved around them. It became harder to keep hold of Keal's belt. Just as he moved right to avoid a jutting piece of rebar, Keal went left. David came off his feet, and he sailed into the rebar. It scraped his arm, but he had no time to think of the pain. He scrambled, his feet out of control, then pedaled again beside

Keal. Xander was having just as much trouble. He jerked at David's pants, causing David's hips to shift this way and that, totally out of sync with his upper torso.

David was about to release his grip on Keal when Dad yelled, "Stay together! Don't let go!"

They continued that way, a train now off the tracks but still locomoting forward—emphasis on *loco*: didn't that mean *crazy* in Spanish? Yeah, *crazy*. Down, down, closer and closer to the creatures waiting for them.

Keal angled a different direction, toward the outer edge of the creatures' camp. Most likely, David knew, Keal wasn't trying to prevent a collision with the creatures but was following the tug of the items.

Fine with me.

The creatures noticed the shift and started jogging to intercept them.

Thirty seconds, David guessed. Half a minute until they met: rocks, teeth, claws, and all.

A gunshot startled him. He tumbled, catching sight of the pistol raised in Keal's hand, aimed at the sky. His feet were gone, left behind. He fell. Xander came down on David, crushing him against a jagged rock. His cast hit the ground. Agony, like an electrical current, radiated into his shoulder.

Keal jerked to a stop. He reached back, grabbed David's shirt, and hoisted him up.

David felt Xander rising behind him.

"Let's move!" Keal said. He fired another shot into the air.

The creatures responded. Several were already running away. The others were disappearing behind slabs of broken buildings, into cubbyholes.

"The pull's strong now," Dad said. "The portal must be just ahead."

Keal slid up onto the hood of a rusted, crumpled car, pulling David with him. He dropped down on the other side. The train followed.

Only one creature remained. Another gunshot sent it scrambling between two huge sections of what looked to David like a street, only standing on end.

Yeah, he thought. *We're doing it.*

The four of them scrambled over larger and larger clumps of debris. Finally, they jumped down onto a flat area, cleared of trash. A big circle of rocks in the middle marked a fire pit. Only gray and black ashes filled the space inside.

"Over here," Keal said, tugging David—and, in turn, Xander and Dad—across the open area.

A movement caught David's eye. He turned in time to see the bold creature lurch into the clearing from the other side. The thing held a spear over his head, aiming it—and wild, fiery eyes—directly at David.

CHAPTER

Six

The creature hoisted the long weapon back over his shoulder.

"Keal!" Xander yelled. "Shoot him!"

Keal swung the pistol around and pulled the trigger. *Click. Click. Click.*

"Aahh!" he said. "I took out a bullet for safety!" He jabbed his fingers into his shirt pocket. "It's not here. I lost it."

David watched the creature shuffle forward. He kept shifting his aim to each of them in turn, as if deciding which to kill.

Who? David thought. *Who's going to get it?*

"Move!" Keal yelled. He leaped.

Xander went the other direction. Connected to both of them, David jerked sideways, right, then left. And the four of them didn't go either way; their evasive maneuvers canceled each other out.

David let go of Keal's belt and dropped straight down.

A flash of white shot out from the rubble at the perimeter and crashed into the man with the spear. A second creature was on top of the spearman, bringing him down. Their rescuer ended up on top. He slashed his hands at Spear-man and looked up. Scar tissue ran from his hairline, skipped over his eye, and continued down his cheek. It was the creature David had saved from Keal's first shot. Its eyes locked on David's.

David nodded. He scrambled up, grabbing Keal's pants. "Go! Go!"

They ran across the clearing.

Tugging along behind Keal, David looked back at the creatures. The bold one slammed the side of the spear into the other's head. The one who'd saved them went down, appearing to be out cold. Spear-man turned toward them again.

"Faster," David said. "Keal, run!"

Spear-man stepped forward and almost fell. The other creature had a grip on his ankle. Spear-man spun and thrust the weapon down, nicking the downed man's calf. He howled, baring a mouth of bent and missing teeth. He grabbed the javelin. Spear-man tugged but couldn't free it. He let it go and ran for them.

"Let go of me, David," Keal said, handing him the blanket.

"But, why——?"

Keal charged toward their attacker.

David let his fingers slip off the belt. He said, "Dad?"

His father held up his hand, telling him to hold on.

Before Keal and the creature met, Keal ducked low. He seized the man by the knees, rose, and flipped him over his head. The creature landed on his back, hitting so hard David winced. Keal leaped backward, planting one foot on either side of his opponent. He dropped, aiming his knee at the man's chest. The creature rolled against Keal's leg, surprisingly fast. As Keal's knee struck the ground, the creature slid out from under him and sprang from the ground, wrapping his arms and legs around Keal's head and chest.

Dad hurried past Xander and David. "Let's go. This way." He pointed. The edges of the blanket in David's hands stretched and flapped in the same direction.

David grabbed his arm. "We can't leave him!"

Dad appeared unsure. Keal yelled, and all eyes returned to the fight.

The creature was biting the top of Keal's head. Dad started for them. Keal planted a fist in the creature's ear. It was the fist that held the tam-o'-shanter; David wondered if the cap would pad the blow, but the creature's head snapped away. He fell off Keal and thudded onto the ground. The creature gripped its head and rolled back and forth.

Keal ran to the group, collected the blanket, and said, "Okay, then. Belts?"

They held on to each other again, and Keal led them across the clearing. He climbed on top of a chest-high lump of asphalt, reached back, and yanked David up. They dropped to the other side. Xander lost his grip on David's pants and spilled over the rock. He rose and moved just as Dad's feet came down.

The butterfly net flew out of Dad's hand and sailed through the air. As Dad reached for it, it hit Xander's back, flipped over his shoulder, struck David in the head, and kept going—until it disappeared a few seconds later.

The portal! David saw it now. It presented itself as a shimmering oval that seemed to project in midair a translucent image of a room: wood floor, finished walls, a bench.

Keal plunged into it. His body wavered, as though seen through the heated exhaust of a jet engine. Then David went through. Blinding light. A gust of wind. He landed on his knees, cracking them hard. He fell and shot forward. He was still gripping Keal, who was scrambling up onto the bench, apparently to get out of the way.

David didn't feel Xander on his back. Hanging from Keal, his legs dangling on the floor, he craned his head around.

His brother leaped through the portal. He kept coming,

tripped over David, and ran headfirst into the closed door that led to the hallway.

"Oww!" Xander yelped. He bounded back, holding his head.

Dad burst into the room and slammed into Xander, shoving him once again into the door.

Groaning, Xander turned and slid down the door until he sat on the floor.

"Sorry," Dad said, stepping over David's legs. He leaned to examine Xander's forehead. "You okay?"

"I *was*," Xander said, burying his face in his hands. "Until we got home."

David pulled himself up by Keal's belt and plopped down on the bench. "I thought we were dead meat," he said. He rubbed his face where the butterfly net had smacked it, then caressed his cast, though a lot of good that did. He closed his eyes and let out a heavy breath.

Keal lowered himself beside David. He set the pistol on the bench and patted his chest. Then he reached into a pocket and fished out a bullet, holding it up for David to see. "Wrong pocket," he said shyly.

"Some safety trick," David said. He grinned at Keal. "I'm kind of glad it worked out the way it did."

Keal set the bullet down. He rubbed the top of his head and brought back a bloody palm. Long gouges—claw marks—ran the length of his forearm.

"Better get something for those," Dad said. "Who knows what kind of diseases those creatures have."

"Let's rest first," Keal said, closing his eyes.

Dad sat on the other side of David, nudging him. "Scoot over, fatty."

"Hey," David said, thankful to be saying something that didn't have anything to do with life and death. "You always tell me I could use more meat on my bones. I—" He stopped. "Did you just hear something? Like a scream?"

Dad scowled at him, listening. "No, I . . ." He turned. "The portal's still open." A gusty sound was coming from it. "It always shuts. When the last item comes through, it always closes."

"Keal," Xander said. "Where's the tam-o'-shanter? The cap you had?"

Keal cracked an eye. "What?" He looked at his hands, seeming surprised to find them empty.

Frowning, Dad stood. He reached for the door.

"No, I meant in the hall," David said "I thought I heard—"

There it was again: muffled by the door and the windy sound of the open portal—a high, terrified scream.

Dad spun, eyes wide. "Toria!"

Xander reached up for the handle, turning and rising.

Dad took a step for the hallway door.

Behind him, a shadow darkened the portal. Spear-man leaped through.

CHAPTER

Seven

David cried out.

The creature—Spear-man—landed on Dad's back and clung to it. The tam-o'-shanter fell from the creature's hand. Before it hit the floor, the portal door slammed shut.

Dad staggered forward just as Xander got the hallway door open. Dad rushed through, turned, and rammed the creature into a wall. Spear-man held on, scratching at Dad's face and neck.

Keal grabbed the gun, opened the cylinder, and dropped in

31

the bullet he'd found. He stepped into the hallway and tried to get a bead on the creature.

David and Xander darted out of the antechamber. They dodged past Dad, the thing on his back, and Keal's swinging, gun-packing arm.

Cold air blew against David's arms, the back of his neck. He looked behind him. "Xander," he said, "the door."

Another antechamber door, a few feet from them, was open. Light and rainy wind poured from it. The family's aluminum ladder lay on the floor, across the doorway.

"Get away from it," Xander said. He pulled his brother toward the fighting men.

The pistol stopped swaying and locked on the creature's head.

Dad reached out and closed his fingers around the gun barrel. "Not him," he said through clenched teeth. "*Him!*" He pointed down the hall.

At the landing, Nana clung to the wall. Her legs were stretched out into the hall, shaking six inches above the floor. Toria had her arms wrapped around one leg. She turned a wet face toward them.

"Help!"

Beyond Toria and Nana, standing on the landing, was Taksidian.

The lights flickered, turning the scene on and off.

"Keal," Dad said, "I got this guy." As if to make his point, he heaved back against the wall again, crushing the creature. "Get *that* one!"

Keal shifted his aim to Taksidian. "Back off!" he yelled. "Get out of here! Now!"

Instead, Taksidian lowered his gaze and kicked at Nana's hand.

Keal fired. A small explosion erupted from the wall a hand's breadth from Taksidian's face. The lights flicked off. When they sprang on a second later, Taksidian was gone.

Nana sailed toward them, skimming over the runner that traversed the length of the hall. Toria came with her. Then, when they'd closed half the distance between them, Toria lost her grip and spun away.

"Grab her!" Dad yelled. "Grab my mother!"

Keal dropped the pistol and rushed forward. He dropped down on Nana, encircling his massive arms around her waist. Both of them continued moving toward the open door—not so quickly, though.

"That's why the portal's open," Xander said. "It wants her." He moved past Dad, who was holding the creature's hand to keep it from clawing his face and leaning his head away from the snapping mouth.

Xander threw himself down. Nana crashed into him. Her legs went over him, and he grabbed them. The three of them— Xander, Nana, and Keal—slid, much more slowly now, toward the antechamber.

"Dad," David said, "what do we do?"

"I don't know, Dae." He rammed the creature against the wall. "It wants her." For a moment, he stopped struggling with the creature. Spear-man nipped at Dad's head, then bit his back. Dad hissed, gritted his teeth. "Wait," he said. "It wants *someone.*"

"Who?" Then David got it. "The creature. Give the portal *him.* Will that work?"

Dad staggered toward the antechamber door. "Worth a try."

The creature glared over Dad's shoulder at the light coming through the door. David thought he saw the anger in his eyes change to fear. Spear-man began writhing furiously. He pounded on Dad's arm and head. He wanted off, but now it was Dad holding him on.

David backed away, past the open door.

The creature squirmed and fought. Dad lost his grip, and the man fell to the floor. Immediately he began kicking at the floor, trying to propel himself away, but Dad grabbed his ankles and pulled him toward the door.

"The ladder, Dae," Dad said. "Hurry."

Nana, Xander, and Keal were inching closer, seconds from running into the creature's flailing hands.

David dropped to his knees. He pulled on the rungs. The ladder glided over the floor . . . then it hit the wall at the end of the hallway. It still blocked the opening. Dad was too close for David to flip it down or swing it away from the doorway.

He pushed it the other direction. When the end of the ladder reached him, he gripped it and pushed, shoving it past the doorway. Leaning into the light, the cold, wet wind stung his face.

"Got it!" he yelled. "Go, go, do it!"

Dad swung around, heaving the man's legs into the antechamber. The creature screeched in terror, spun, and clawed at the floor. He zipped into the room as though he were on a waterslide.

"David, back away!" Dad yelled.

Too late: the creature's bony fingers wrapped around David's ankle. David's legs, hips, body followed his foot. His shoulder smacked against the opposite jamb. Then he was coasting on the icy floor, bathed in light.

"Daaaad!" he screamed. He felt the wind grab him, cold and powerful.

Dad lunged for him. His hands came down on David's. *No, no, they didn't!* They came down on the floor where David's hands had been a half second before. David was moving too fast.

Dad scrambled to catch up, reaching, reaching. His eyes were white orbs with blue dots at their center; his pupils were pinpricks in the bright light. His mouth was moving, but David could hear nothing but the howl of the wind.

He went through, splashing down into water so cold he thought his heart would stop. But of course it didn't. It pounded hard and fast, pumping blood up to his panicked brain. He squinted against light shining in his eyes, just as bright and blinding as it had appeared from the other side.

The portal shimmered above him. It showed him a ghostly image of Dad, rising from the antechamber floor, diving for the portal. The door slammed, as fast and silent as a flying arrow.

The portal dissolved into water droplets and swirled away.

CHAPTER

eight

WEDNESDAY, 6:56 P.M.

Xander felt the pull on his grandmother stop. Her body went limp. Cautiously, he released her legs. When she didn't try to sail over him, he slid out from under her.

"Is it over?" Keal said.

"I think so." Xander was relieved to see Nana's back rising and falling. It was only then that he admitted to himself that a small part of him feared that she had died. He crawled to her head and laid his hand against her hair. He whispered, "Nana, are you all right?"

She turned her face to him. Her eyes were wet and blood-shot. Since he'd last seen her an hour before, she seemed to have aged years. She blinked at him.

"Yes, dear," she said. "Nothing I haven't been through before, in one way or another." She smiled.

Xander shook his head.

She looked back at Keal, kneeling beside her. "Thank you," she said.

"Next time we dance," he said, "it's my turn to lead."

Nana rose, shifted, and sat cross-legged. She spotted Toria, standing frozen in the hallway, both hands covering her mouth.

Nana spread her arms wide. "And you," she said. "My hero."

Toria dropped her hands, revealing an ear-to-ear grin. She came running.

Xander hiked himself up and went to the antechamber. "She's okay, Dad," he said. "The pull stopped. What'd you do?"

Then he saw that his father was wearing what looked like a bulky bulletproof vest. He was hastily cinching a series of straps around the vest and tying knots in them.

Xander's guts suddenly felt hollow. He scanned the small room, quickly leaned through the door, and looked up and down the hall. "Dad?" He swallowed. It felt like a marble going down. "Dad, where's Dae?"

Dad glanced at him. "He went over."

"What? Why? On purpose?"

Dad shook his head. "It was my fault. I was trying to get that creature through the portal. It grabbed him." He snatched another item from the hooks. It appeared to be a pair of suspenders. He draped it over his neck.

Xander grabbed his arm. "Dad, we'll get him. He's been over alone before."

Dad turned to him. "This time it's different. It's not even so much that he was *pulled* over, against his will. It's . . . I don't know, how it felt. It brought back a memory, a horrible memory."

"Of Mom? When she was taken?"

"Of when *my* mother—Nana—was taken." Dad wiped a hand over his face. "The light. My trying to do something and not being able to. Arms reaching out to me." His frown deepened. "His eyes, Xander. They were so scared."

"Dad, we can go get him together," Xander said. "You and me, it'll be better that way. We can—"

"No," Dad said. "Not this time. Listen, if I don't come back, don't come after me. It'll be too late."

"Don't—?" Xander shook his head. "That's crazy. You'd better believe I'm coming. For you and David? Come on!"

Dad nodded toward something on the bench by the door, and Xander followed it with his eyes.

"Oh, no."

Dad picked it up. "Gotta go," he said. He wrapped an arm around Xander. "I love you." He crossed to the portal door and opened it.

Light filled the room. Cold air blew in.

"It doesn't matter," Xander said. "If you're not back in a half hour, I'm coming after you. You hear?"

"Don't," Dad said, and stepped through.

Xander watched him hit water. He went under, then resurfaced.

"You'd better come back!" Xander called.

The door slammed closed. He stared at it for a long time, but he wasn't seeing the door. He was seeing the item his father had picked up. It was a life buoy, a white ring for throwing to people in deep water. Pools had them. And ships, like the one from which this particular life buoy came—as indicated by the black-stenciled lettering on it: **R.M.S. TITANIC**.

CHAPTER

nine

Edward King was on the deck of the ship, but he was also in the icy waters of the Atlantic Ocean. The ship was listing, angled like one of the arms on the letter *V*. Its bow was underwater, its stern high in the air. He was just below the intersection of water and ship. While the life vest from the antechamber kept him on the surface, the toes of his shoes skimmed the deck.

The tragedy of the *Titanic* had always fascinated him—the

arrogance of the ship's designers and owners. Not arrogance—
hubris, a word not taught enough in schools. It meant excessive
pride or self-confidence. In Greek mythology, it resulted from
scorning the gods, and the gods in turn unleashed their powers
to bring the offenders down.

He could not think of an event in modern history that
better illustrated the concept. The owners called the *Titanic*
"unsinkable." They had been so boastful of this belief that
half the passengers refused to board the lifeboats when the
crew told them to. It was only when the decks began flooding
and the ship's listing could no longer be ignored that panic
had set in, starting a mad scramble.

They were all gone now, the lifeboats. He knew most of
them were less than half-full, leaving fifteen hundred people
to die. He could see a good number of these people scrambling toward the stern, climbing higher and higher, hoping the
ship would stop its plunge to the bottom before the water
reached them.

Mr. King knew better.

He began swimming toward the exposed deck, twenty feet
in front of him. The surface was littered with scraps of paper,
clothing that hadn't yet sunk, a child's doll. He pushed
through it all, trying to keep his mind from thinking that all
the clutter paled in comparison to the number of corpses that
would soon fill the ocean. Before emerging from the water, he
realized he could stand. He'd kept hold of the life preserver

he'd brought from the antechamber. Now he slipped an arm through it and rested it on his shoulder. He trudged out of the water, feeling the deck slipping down under his feet like a stepless escalator.

He remembered that the stern's propellers had risen out of the water at 2:10 in the morning—which they had already done. By 2:20, the entire ship sank below the surface . . . or rather, *would* sink. He had fewer than ten minutes to find David.

He looked at his watch. It was on Pinedale time: 7:00, exactly. The second hand had stopped.

"David!" he yelled. "David!"

The stern rose higher. People screamed. Chairs, luggage, bodies tumbled down the deck toward him. The water rose up behind him, touching his ankles, reaching his calves.

He leaned forward, climbed.

A light, shining on him from an empty lifeboat stanchion, sputtered and went out. Some of the bulbs clinging to an eave running the length of the deck exploded under a surge of electrical current. The rest of them flickered, then went black.

Mr. King looked past the railing at the vast ocean, black under a moonless sky. He thought he could make out a handful of lifeboats bobbing around like giant bodies. He could only hope David was on one of them. If he had come over before the final boats had left, they would have taken him, a child, wouldn't they?

"David!" he called.

A faint answer reached him: "Dad?"

"David?"

"Dad!"

It was coming from the stern. He ran—as quickly as the rising deck allowed him to. He grabbed the railing to pull himself along, pull himself up.

"David!" Mr. King stared up at the people crowded on the stern. Many were jumping or falling over the side, plunging into the water sixty feet below.

Lord, he thought, *let me reach my son. Let us find the portal home together. And if that's not to be, let us die together.*

"Dad?"

The small voice was close.

"Dae? I'm here! Where are you?"

"Here!"

He climbed. He reached a spot where a doorway jutted out from the *Titanic's* massive center. Beside it a circular vent, like a large candy cane, protruded from the deck. David clung to the upward side of the vent, hugging it. He was wet and shivering violently. His hair was plastered to his skull. His eyes were closed. They opened, took in his father, and his quivering lips bent into a smile.

He said, "Is that . . . is that really you?" His smile faltered, breaking his dad's heart.

Mr. King broke from the railing, almost slid away on the

deck, and grabbed the vent. He shuffled around to get his arm over David's back. The boy's trembling muscles reverberated into his dad's arm, into his body.

"It's me, Dae," he said. "I'm here."

David hitched in a breath. He started to weep.

Mr. King closed his eyes, wishing none of this for his boy. He squeezed him. "Shhhh."

"I . . ." David said. "I landed on the deck when I came through, but it was already underwater. I got out as fast as I could. But I'm so *cold*."

More than the temperature. Shock. Fear. "I know," his father said.

"There was a lifeboat," David said. "I wanted to get on, but they wouldn't let me. They just kept lowering it. They wouldn't let me on."

"It's okay, son. I have something better. I have items from the antechamber, Dae. They'll lead us home."

David blinked at him. "Really?"

He nodded and looked around. "We just have to get away from the ship. It's going to break in two any minute." *And right about where we are,* he thought, but didn't say.

"But . . . but . . ."

"What, son?"

"Mom," David said. His eyes were as wide as they had been when the spearman had pulled him into this world.

"What about her? We'll find her. We will. But we have to get back home first."

"It's why I stopped here," David said. "Dad, look!" He pointed to the wall beside him. Scrawled in what looked like lipstick was the King family mascot: Bob.

CHAPTER

ten

WEDNESDAY, 7:07 P.M.

Toria's arms were starting to ache from hugging Nana so
tightly. She pushed her face into her grandmother's neck, getting it wet with tears. She didn't want to cry, but the more she
tried to stop, the harder she sobbed. She hitched in ragged
breaths, then let them out in wet mumblings: "I was so scared
. . . I thought you were gone . . . and, and then that man
showed up . . ."

When Dad had burst into the hallway, that horrible thing on his back, she'd been too stunned to call out at first. Finally, she had, and somehow Dad made it all better, as he did so often. Now that Nana was okay, it struck her just how weird her father's appearance was: Where had he come from, and were Keal and David and Xander with him? How had Keal gotten a gun? And what was that hideous creature on his back, and where had *it* come from?

That made her curious: where was it now?

She sniffed, said, "I'm just glad you're all right." She lifted her face and brushed away the strands of Nana's hair clinging to it. Then she straightened to her full height, wiping at her eyes.

Nana smiled at her. She stroked Toria's cheek and said, "You're only nine? Are you *sure?*" She shook her head. "My son certainly raised a fighter." She gripped Toria by the shoulders to look at her square on. "Toria, *thank you.*"

Toria smiled, a little shyly. She didn't feel like she'd done anything special. What was she supposed to do, watch the house eat Nana? Her eyes shifted to the open antechamber. The skin at the back of her neck tingled. If the doorway was a mouth, she wondered if it had been fed; is that what had made it stop pulling at Nana?

She spun her head around and saw Keal in the hallway, groaning as he rose to his feet. Where was everyone else?

"Dad?" she called to the door. "Xander! David!"

The creature wasn't screeching anymore, as it had been doing between bites at Dad's head and neck. Where was it? Where were *they*?

Nana was looking from her to the door, back to her. Toria could tell she was getting scared too.

"Dad!" Toria said.

A shadow slid over the door frame, and Xander stuck his head out. He frowned at her. "Dad went over," he said. "David too."

"Why?" Toria and Nana said in unison.

"I guess that creature pulled Dae over. Dad went after him."

He looked *between* Toria and Nana, not at either of them. Toria knew her brother enough to know there was something he wasn't saying.

"What else, Xander?" she said. "What happened?"

"I'll go," Keal's deep voice said behind her. He looked ready to do it, to go do whatever had to be done.

"No," Xander said. "I promised Dad we'd wait."

There's that look in his eyes again, Toria thought. *He's not telling everything.*

Keal looked over his shoulder. He stiffened. "Hey, what's the wheelchair doing up here?" he said. "Where's Jesse?" He turned wide eyes on them. "Anyone seen him? Jesse?"

"He was downstairs," Toria said. "He came to help when Nana started to get pulled away. He tried to stop her from going, but I guess he had to let go."

"I thought someone was with him," Nana said. "When Jesse let go, someone else was there, in the hall. I thought it was you or Eddie. I was so panicked, I didn't think about it until now."

Then it dawned on Toria: "Taksidian!" she said.

Keal started for the staircase. "Downstairs?"

"By my bedroom."

"Wait!" Xander said, coming out of the antechamber. "He might still be here . . . waiting." He looked back into the small room. "It can't change, right? The portal can't go away until they come back, can it?"

"I thought you knew that stuff!" Toria said.

He nodded. "It'll be okay." He bit his lower lip. "Just in case, could you and Nana sit in here? Just for a minute?"

"Xander!" Toria yelled. "It tried to *eat* her!"

"Never mind," he said, starting for Keal.

Toria grabbed his wrist. "What about Dad and Dae?" she said.

"I told you—"

"What else?" She raised her eyebrows.

His worried look grew deeper, became something like pain. He said, "It was wet and cold over there. I could feel it blowing in, and I saw Dad land in water."

Toria nodded. She remembered the bitter chill blowing in when she'd approached the antechamber. He tried to shake off her hand, but she clenched it tighter. She said, "And?"

"One of the items he took," her brother said. "It was a life preserver. It had the word *Titanic* on it."

His eyes found Nana's, and Toria knew what he wanted: he hoped she would say something like, *Oh, that old thing? That's nothing. I've seen it before. Leads to a museum.*

Nana didn't say that. She just stared, her face muscles tight.

Xander pulled himself free. "I'll be right back." And he ran.

When Keal saw him coming, he disappeared through the landing doorway to shoot down the stairs.

"Nana?" Toria said.

"It'll be all right, dear." Her eyes were on the antechamber. They didn't match her words. They said, *Maybe it won't be all right. Maybe nothing will be all right ever again.*

eleven

"We can't stay here, David," Dad said. "The ship's going to break in half any minute now."

David's teeth clattered. His entire body trembled with cold. It felt like he'd been sprayed down and put in a freezer. Dad didn't look much better. "But, D-D-Dad . . . B-B-Bob!"

They both looked at it. Smeared, shaky, incomplete.

"You," Dad said, "you didn't draw it?"

"It w-w-was Mom. Had-had to be." *Or Nana*, David

thought. Had she ever been here? Had she been putting Bob on things for the same reason they had started do it, to let someone know she'd been there, to help them find her?

"If it was Mom," Dad said, "she would have gotten into a lifeboat by now." He stood, pulling David up with him. "We have to go. When the ship breaks up, it sinks right away. We can't be on it or even near it." He tugged David toward the railing. "Hold this." He gave him a life preserver. "It's from the house. If we get separated, it'll lead you to the portal home."

David slipped the ring over his cast. He grabbed his father's life vest, one hand on the sleeve hole, the other on the collar. "Don't leave me," he said. His breath turned into a cloud between them.

"I won't." Dad wrapped an arm around David's waist and lifted him over the railing. "We'll go together."

David kept holding on. It occurred to him that Dad might throw him over, then go back into the ship, looking for Mom. The prospect of being alone in the water with Dad inside a sinking ship, terrified him. But as soon as David was on the other side, his feet on the edge of the deck, Dad stepped over. He looked down. The water was twenty feet below, churning against the ship, rushing onto the decks below them.

Dad said, "On three . . ."

CHAPTER

twelve

WEDNESDAY, 7:09 P.M.

Xander moved down the stairs, right behind Keal. The man tromped over the collapsed walls, making them rock and rattle.

Xander followed, remembering how Phemus—the huge brute who'd taken Mom—had pushed down the walls like they were dominoes. Then he'd come after them—Xander, David, and Toria. If Keal had not come and fought Phemus off, they'd be dead for sure.

So many close calls. He didn't know if he should be angry that the house and whatever made it tick were out to get them—or glad that it seemed Someone was protecting them.

"Jesse?" Keal called and rounded the corner into the main second-floor hallway. "Jesse!"

Xander felt his spine grow cold. That last call wasn't an inquiry; it was a cry of anguished concern. In a movie, it was the scream that signaled serious trouble. He didn't have to see it to know Keal had found Jesse, and it wasn't good.

He stopped before he reached the corner. He pressed his palms against the wall, lowered his head, and closed his eyes.

Breathe, he thought. *Just breathe.*

Keal's footsteps pounded down the hall. "Jesse! Jesse!"

No reply.

Xander listened . . . He should be there, helping any way he could—watching out for Taksidian while Keal tended to Jesse. But Xander didn't want to know what had happened. Yesterday David had said, "We need a *break*, Xander. Ever since we moved in, it's been one bad thing after another. Why can't something good happen for once?"

He knew now exactly how David had felt. It had taken him a little longer to reach that point, but he was there. Oh man, was he there.

We do need a break, Dae, he thought. *You were right.* He realized something: whatever this was he was feeling—a panic attack? a closing down? frustrated paralysis?—it had little to do with the fear of seeing what had happened to Jesse. It wasn't even brought on by all the things he, Xander, had been through.

It was David. Xander feared for him, missed him. He was sorry for all the things his brother was going through. In the *Mission: Impossible* movies, Tom Cruise was too cool to be threatened into action, but as soon as a loved one was in danger, everything changed. Torture was nothing next to someone you cared about being tortured.

"Xander?" Keal yelled. "Xander!"

Shake it off, Xander thought. *Get tough. You can do it!*

"Xander!"

Xander pushed off the wall. He staggered, found his feet, went around the corner.

Keal was leaning over Jesse. The old man was on the floor where a railing separated the hallway from the foyer below. As Xander approached, he saw a red pool spreading out from Jesse's body.

Keal glanced up. "I think he's been stabbed."

"Is he——?" Xander stopped.

Jesse's eyes were shut, but his mouth hung open. His natural paleness had hued to bluish-white. Veins coursed over his forehead, and age spots covered his bald scalp. The wispy gray hair from his temples and the back of his head fanned out behind him. He looked like a rag doll tossed out with the trash.

"Is he dead?" Xander stepped over the pool and knelt by Jesse's hip, across from Keal.

So much blood, Xander thought. It soaked the old man's shirt, obscuring the plaid pattern on his shoulder and chest. Xander could smell it now, a little like raw hamburger. For a moment he thought he was going to puke. He swallowed and forced himself to handle it. Sometimes that's just what you had to do: handle it.

"He's got a pulse," Keal said, "but it's weak. He's lost a lot of blood. I have to get him to a hospital."

"I'll call 911." Xander patted his pants, looking for his phone.

"No time," Keal said. He pushed his arms under Jesse and lifted. Jesse's head flopped back; his mouth yawned wider. One arm dangled.

Xander grabbed Jesse's hand. It was bony and felt wrong, unnatural. It was so slick with blood it could have been skinned. He laid it on top of Jesse's chest.

Keal carried Jesse down the stairs. His gaze never left Jesse's face, as though his *watching* were a lifeline that kept the old man from slipping away. He hit the foyer, effortlessly flung open the door, and rushed out.

Xander leaned against the newel at the top of the stairs. He wanted to collapse right there, just fall to the floor, curl up into a ball, and pretend none of this was happening.

No, he thought. *Move, start moving. Do something. Anything.*

But he was achy—in his mind and every part of his body.

Aaahh! He pictured himself screaming like that painting,

the long-faced screamer that had become a popular Halloween mask after being used in the *Scream* movies.

If I'm *feeling this way, imagine how David feels. He was beat yesterday, then all this happens. Taksidian coming at us through the closet, the showdown in the clearing, finding the ruins of Los Angeles—of humankind—and those creatures coming after us. He's younger than I am, and . . . and I'm here and he's fighting for his life on the* Titanic! *Xander, you are such a baby!*

He forced himself to move. Heading for the stairs to the third floor, he glanced back and stopped. Jesse had left a mess on the floor: himself spilled out all over it . . . but something more.

Xander went back to the blood. A trail of it snaked away, running to the steps and down each one. It wasn't this that had caught his attention, however. There was something on the floor near where Xander had knelt, where Jesse's seemingly skinned hand had rested. It was a message, symbols, written in blood:

Clearly, the first one was a house . . . or a spearhead. Then the letter *T*, or an ax, followed by . . . SpongeBob's teeth? Like in *Indiana Jones and the Kingdom of the Crystal Skull*, their survival might depend on figuring out what the pictograms meant. Not that Xander thought for a second that there was anything fun or entertaining about the symbols: he couldn't imagine what it must have taken Jesse to draw them, stabbed, bleeding out. They must be important, even though they made no sense. He hurried to the room they had dubbed their Mission Control Center, and came back with a pad of paper and a pen. He copied the symbols, trying to be as precise as he could. He did it twice, just to be sure.

The blood on his hands was sticky. It left his fingerprints in red in the margins of the paper.

A bloodied document with cryptic symbols from a dying man, he thought. *We're living a movie.*

Two weeks ago, he would have added *Yee-haw!* But this was a story he didn't like so much, one of those films that doesn't end happily and sends the audience shuffling out with long faces.

He returned to the MCC and dropped the pad on the desk beside the computer monitor. That task completed, his thoughts returned to Dad and David. He needed to be in the antechamber, waiting for their return. He left the room and tromped over the fallen walls. At the base of the stairs, he spotted Toria helping Nana maneuver out of the crooked hallway and onto the landing. He started up, then stopped.

"Wait there," he said. "I have to take care of something."

"Xander," Toria said, "Nana needs to lie down."

"Gimme a minute. I'll be right back." He ran back to Jesse's blood, pooled and drizzled and smeared on the floor. It would do Toria and Nana no good to see that. He darted into the bathroom and drenched a towel under the tub's faucet, then dropped it onto the worst of the blood. He swirled it around then carried it, dripping, to the tub. He squeezed it out. He remembered that in *Psycho*, Alfred Hitchcock had used chocolate syrup for blood because brown looked better in black-and-white than red did. *This* was red, and it wrenched at his guts more than any horror movie had ever done.

He went back and forth three more times, swabbing the blood from the hardwood floor. The thin layer of blood that made up the symbols had dried, and he had to scrub to remove them.

"Xander?" Toria called. She was out of sight, but closer than she should have been.

"Just a minute," Xander said. "Stay there!"

"What are you doing?"

"Nothing." He tossed the sopping towel into the tub, then used another towel to wipe up the trail from hallway to bathroom.

He started back toward them. "Okay."

They met at the corner.

Toria squinted up the hall. "What were you doing?"

"Just a little . . ." He almost said *cleanup*, but that would have led to questions he didn't want to answer. He finished by shaking his head.

"You don't look well," Nana said.

Xander shrugged. "I'm worried about Dad and Dae." He looked down. His hands were stained pink, his fingernails outlined in bright red. He put them behind his back.

"Where's Jesse?" Nana said. "Did Keal find him?"

"He was hurt," Xander said. "Unconscious. Keal took him to the hospital." Of course, they had to know *that* much.

"Jesse?" Toria said, tears instantly welling in her eyes.

"Oh," Nana said. "How?"

Xander shook his head. "Something Taksidian did, I guess." Their faces were more than he could bear. "I'd better go wait for Dad and David."

He tried to smile and was pretty sure it turned out looking like he was sucking on a lemon. He brushed passed them and up the flight of stairs.

Wait for them? Is that what he'd said? He had no intention of waiting. His brother needed him. Dad too, even if he didn't know it. Xander wasn't about to sit on his butt while they drowned or froze to death because of a ship that had gone down nearly a hundred years ago.

thirteen

"... Three!"

David and Dad jumped. The mist hanging over the water
and all the darkness made David misjudge where the surface
was. His feet hit it well before he thought they should. He
quickly pulled in a breath, but had only filled his lungs halfway when his head plunged under. Didn't matter: the iciness
of the water made his muscles contract, and he lost all his air
in a single sharp exhale. He was hurting now. How far under,

he didn't know, but it felt like *fathoms*. Black, icy, churning water everywhere. He needed to breathe.

Then he felt Dad tugging at him, pulling him up. He kicked, kicked, fought the impulse to release his grip on his father's life vest and paddle. Dad was doing a better job than he could do. He felt the water rushing past him as they rose.

But oh, he needed air! His chest ached as though a glacier giant had punched his sternum, crushing it.

He opened his eyes. Blackness everywhere. The ocean salt stung; he felt like someone had rubbed sandpaper over his eyeballs. Water slipped into his mouth, and he breathed it into his lungs. He coughed, tried not to breathe in more of the sea—or throw up.

He broke surface. Air! Air! But it seemed as much water went in as the sweet stuff his lungs needed. He coughed and choked. His father lifted him, let him cling to his head as David fought to get oxygen in and water out. Slowly, he caught his breath. He realized he was pushing his father under; the life vests of 1912 weren't the buoyancy rock stars they were in his time. He lowered himself down, off Dad's head, deeper into the water.

A white cloth—it might have been a tablecloth or bedsheet—floated like a drowned ghost beside them. The little girl's doll Dad had seen on the deck bobbed up and down an arm's reach away. He felt a lot like that doll: totally helpless, at the mercy of the ocean.

"I'm freezing," David said. It wasn't the kind of cold that

was content to brush against your skin. His organs felt cold, his stomach and heart. He imagined his bones becoming brittle with the cold. Something was going to bump into him, and he would shatter.

"The water's twenty-eight degrees," Dad said. "The average person can last no more than twenty minutes in water this cold."

"Twenty m-m-minutes," David chattered. Shorter than an episode of *Avatar: The Last Air Bender*. "We'd b-b-better find the p-p-portal fast."

Dad nodded. "We have to get away from the ship before it breaks up and goes under. It might suck us down with it."

They began kicking away.

"Stay close to me," Dad said. "Maybe we can keep each other warm." He blinked water out of his eyes and scowled at David's distressed expression. "What is it?"

"I d-d-don't think I have any w-warmth to share."

"Don't worry about it. Do me a favor, slip through that buoy. Wear it under your arms."

"Hold it for me," David said. Without thinking too hard, because he wouldn't act if he did, he went underwater and shot up through the center of the ring, arms first. With the ring pushing on his armpits, he floated higher in the water than his father. As tight as the ring was around his chest, it was better this way: it kept water from splashing his face and allowed him to get a better grip on Dad's life vest.

Dad continued to swim away from the big ship. He stayed on his side, kicking with both feet and paddling with the underwater hand. The other hand gripped David's ring.

"How's—" Dad said, and spat out a mouthful of water. "How's your cast holding up?"

"It's kind of crumbling," David said. "But it's so cold my arm is numb, so I don't feel anything."

A loud *crack!* filled the air, the sound of a thousand rifles shooting at the same time. Then the sound of crushing metal: a low *eeeeeerrrrrrrrr.*

Dad gaped over David's head at the ship. "It's breaking in two," he said. He began kicking and paddling harder.

David watched as the boards splintered on the deck about halfway up the sloping portion of the ship that was out of the water. The part of the ship above this break began leaning back toward the water in jarring spurts. Passengers who'd been clinging to the farthest reaches of the bow lost their grips on the railings, mounted fixtures, and other people. They either fell over the sides into the water; backward over the bow, striking the propellers; or down the length of the deck, landing on riggings or vents or sliding right into the fissure.

It was like watching people jump to their deaths from a burning building.

He blinked and rubbed water out of his eyes, not believing what he was seeing. About ten feet over the deck, just below the break, a shimmering rectangle had appeared. It was probably nothing most people would even see, just a slight wavering of the light, distorting a section of porthole windows behind it. But David was accustomed to seeing it. He knew what it was.

"Dad," David said, pointing. "That's the portal, isn't it? The way home?"

"Better not be," Dad said. "We can't—"

Then David's mistake became apparent. It wasn't the portal home. It was a new one *from* home. Xander materialized in front of it and dropped toward the deck, feet kicking, arms pinwheeling, mouth and eyes wide open. He appeared to be wearing a white steward's coat, and held something shiny in his left hand. Before hitting the deck, he disappeared from David's line of sight.

CHAPTER

fourteen

"Xander!" Dad yelled.

The ship's bow dropped away from the break quickly now. It splashed into the water, and the entire inverted-V of the ship rose in the air, then settled back down. A giant wave, caused by the crashing bow, rolled toward David and Dad.

"Hold on," Dad said. They rode the swell, rising high in the air. So high, in fact, that David could see the deck where Xander had dropped. His brother was hanging on to a rope, swinging over the wooden planks like a pendulum. The ship was seconds away from completely submerging. If Xander didn't get away, he'd ride it to the ocean floor like a cowboy breaking a steer.

"Xander!" David yelled, but the swell was gone and they were dropping down again.

The ship sank faster, abandoning all pretense of seaworthiness. The section forward of the break plunged. It slipped into the ocean like a snake into a hole.

Xander appeared at the edge of the deck, sliding on his stomach over the planks themselves. Without pausing, he sailed over the edge and fell into the churning sea.

"Get away from the ship, Xander!" Dad yelled. "Xander, swim away!"

The swells made it impossible to spot where he'd gone.

"Dad!" David said, choking on a throatful of saltwater. He coughed, coughed. Dad slapped him on the back—*Is that really supposed to help?* David thought almost automatically. He spat out water, exchanged it for air. Finally he could say, "Dad, do you think Xander knows to get away from the sinking ship? You think he heard us?"

"He's seen *Titanic*, right?" Dad said.

"He's seen *everything!*"

Dad nodded. "It showed how people were pulled under by the suction created when the ship when down. Xander will remember. He'll swim away from it. He will." He sounded more hopeful than sure.

They watched the spot where Xander had hit the water. Just swells and churning sea.

Beyond, the *Titanic* pulled its bow under. The rear section of the ship rose up like a hand grasping for help that wasn't there. Then it plunged straight down, disappearing in seconds.

"Xander!" Dad called.

"What's he doing here, anyway?" David said. "Why'd he—"

It felt as though a hand grabbed him from below and tugged him down. Before he knew it, his head was completely submerged. Water rushed down his throat. He kicked and kicked, paddled his hands, squinted at the bubbles escaping from his nose and mouth, wanted to follow them up. Finally, cold air slapped his cheeks, and he gulped in a breath, then another. Dad grabbed him and pulled him close.

Both of them plunged down, like a fishing bobber, but deeper. They popped up again.

David coughed. Blinked. The fuzzy image of his dad's panicked face floated in front of him. "What's going on? I'm getting pu—"

Pulled under again. He realized the squeezing grip on his torso was the life buoy, the ring around his chest. The very thing that was supposed to keep him afloat was tugging him under. He felt Dad right with him: deep below the surface.

David emerged. Spat water. He hacked it out in a coughing fit. He felt as waterlogged as a towel that had blown into a pool.

"What's going on?" he said. It's pulling me un—"

Under again. He kicked and kicked, waved his arms in the treading-water fashion he'd been taught. His head broke the surface. All he could do was gasp for air. He didn't know how much more he could take. Going under without warning, without breath, time and time again. The short reprieves on the surface were too short, almost torture, teasing his lungs with air, his body with rest.

"Dad?" he said, and took a deep breath. He was afraid to say any more. He wanted his lungs to be ready, full for the next tug.

He had to slip out of the ring. It was the ring. It was pulling him down.

"Go with it, David," Dad said in his ear. He was squeezing him close, pressing his lips right on David's ear. "Next time it pulls you, go with it. Don't fight it."

David jerked his head away. He looked into his father's eyes. "I don't understand. It's under—"

Water washed over his head, and *blast it!* if he didn't swallow a gallon of the salty stuff. He'd promised himself he wouldn't be caught off guard again. He kicked, pulled at Dad, but realized Dad was under too. They both struggled and fought, and eventually David felt the cold, cold night air on his face. He spat and breathed.

Dad was there again, his mouth almost *eating* his ear. "Okay, okay. That one was a surprise," Dad said. "Keep going when it takes you. It's the portal; the items are showing us the way. Look . . ." He pointed.

"W-w-what, the tablecloth, the doll?"

"Yeah," Dad said, excited. "They were beside us a few minutes ago. Now they're way off that way. We should have drifted with them, not in the opposite direction. The items tugged us to the portal. Go with it, Dae."

"But . . . but . . ." David could hardly find the words. "It's *underwater!*"

"Yes, but it can't be too far," Dad said. "The pull is strong. Swim *toward* it. Stop fighting it."

"You . . . you go first," David said. "I'll hold on and follow." He was scared and didn't mind letting it show.

"Listen," Dad said. He held David's chin, pointing their faces at each other. "You go without me. Get home. I'm going to wait for Xander."

"No!" David said. "I'm not leaving you. I'm not leaving Xander." What was it with this family, always separating?

"We've been in the water, what, ten minutes?" Dad said. "I'm having trouble breathing, and I can't feel my hands or feet. You have to be slipping into hyperthermia too, Dae. Maybe worse than me."

David had been too panicked by the constant dunking to notice. He'd chocked up his shallow breathing, his not getting enough air even when he was on the surface long enough to get it, as a side effect of swallowing so much water and being so scared. Hypothermia—freezing to death. Could be that too. His hands and feet had moved when he'd wanted them to, but that was only because they were attached to his arms and legs, heavier muscles that had not yet succumbed to the cold water. He flexed his fingers. They barely moved.

He nodded. His teeth chattered so hard, he thought they might break.

"All right, then," Dad said. "I'll meet you back in the house."

David saw something on a swell over Dad's shoulder: Xander! He was thirty feet away, swimming toward them. He kept looking up, getting his bearings. His arms pumped up and down—a shiny object still in his hand—and his legs kicked. The faint glow of a light somewhere caught the paleness of his face. His eyes sparkled blue, and David noticed his brother's lips were nearly the same color.

Xander opened his mouth wide to gulp in air, a plume of mist billowing out first. His bottom lip trembled so badly, David could *see* it quivering from that distance.

"Look," he said.

Dad did. He reached out and squeezed David's shoulder. "Xander!"

Xander nodded. Something that might have been a smile twisted his lips. He dropped his head to plow ahead. The current or his numbing muscles or *something* caused him to veer off course; if he kept that trajectory, he'd miss them by a mile. Then a strange thing happened. Xander zipped toward them—sideways in the water, still pedaling and paddling with his head down, facing the wrong way. It was like that girl at the beginning of *Jaws* who gets grabbed by the shark and pulled through the water this way and that.

Dad and David watched him come.

"It's the portal," Dad said. "He's got the items from the antechamber. They're pulling him to the portal."

Dad turned to offer David a trembling smile. His eyes flashed wide, and he lurched into David as a breaker—and Xander—crashed into him.

Xander's arms flailed out. The metal thing in his hand slammed into David's forehead. Xander's frightened eyes locked for a second on David's, and he tried to say something, but only water spat out of his mouth. Then he was gone: straight down under the water.

"Xan—!" Dad said. He stuck his face within inches of David's. "Ready?"

David pulled in as much air as his frozen lungs could handle. The ring pulled him like an engine block tied to his body, and he went under. Dad went down right beside him. They ran into Xander, who was coming back up, his limbs twisting and pumping.

He's fighting it, David thought. Though he'd done it himself and understood the impulse, his brother's efforts to reach the surface, to keep them there longer, frustrated him. He pushed down on Xander's shoulder. He grabbed his bicep, and let the tugging take them both down.

I hope Dad's right, he thought. *The portal better be close. And I hope Xander has enough breath to survive the trip.*

Xander clawed at him. His fingers found David's face. They squeezed and scratched.

David tried to turn away.

Something hit them. At first David was sure the *Titanic* had somehow returned to the surface, lurched in the water, and struck the struggling Kings. Then he realized it was he, Dad, and Xander doing the striking. They had reached the portal door.

CHAPTER

fifteen

They fell into the antechamber in a cascade of water.

David remembered thinking that Spear-man, being sucked into the portal, looked like he was shooting down a water-slide. This was *exactly* a waterslide: fast, wet, with a landing that flipped them into the air.

Tumbling, David caught a glimpse of a wave slapping the antechamber's hallway door shut. Then the ceiling light flashed past. More water hit his face, forcing his eyes closed. His back slammed into the floor.

A body—David thought it was Xander—hit the floor in a gush of water and kept coming, right into his head. Another body—had to be Dad—tumbled down beside them.

The water kept pouring, churning over them, making them flip and swivel. It was like the time he'd lost his balance in the surf at Santa Monica Beach. The water pushed them into the antechamber's hallway door, against the bench, into each other.

David forced an eye open. Water rushed through the portal in a solid rectangle. Then the door slammed shut. The water splashed down and was done.

Silence . . . except for their breathing—deep, exhausted panting. And coughing—wet, miserable hacking.

David's back was pressed to the floor. His legs were bent at the hips; they rose straight up along the hallway door. Water dripped off his sneakers onto his bare belly: his shirt was bunched up under his arms and over his chest. His right arm was wedged under the shirt, and he felt his heart pounding like he'd sprinted through a marathon.

His eyes stung. They felt swollen and too large for his sockets, so he kept his lids closed. He remembered a song Dad liked: "Doctor, My Eyes," he thought it was called. It was about a guy who suddenly couldn't see, and the singer wondered if it was because of all the sad things he'd seen.

I could write that song, he thought. *But I better not be blind. Yeah, that's just what I need now.*

He snapped his eyes open. The bulb on the ceiling, inside a wire basket to keep it from breaking, shot white spears into his head. He clamped his eyes closed again.

Okay, easy does it.

He cracked his lids just enough to see through his eyelashes. Dad sat on the floor to his right, leaning his head back against the wall. His chest rose and fell with almost cartoon exaggeration.

David shifted his gaze. Xander's head was pushed up against him. His legs stretched up to the bench, where his feet rested. His teeth chattered like Morse code.

Xander spoke, the cold clinging to his words. "Are . . . are we al-al-alive?"

"I'm t-t-too cold to be d-d-dead," David said.

Xander tried to laugh, but it quickly turned into a series of coughs.

Wind blew in from under the portal door. It swirled around the room, buffeting their clothes and hair. Drops of water filled the air. Then the wind and the water whooshed under the crack beneath the door and were gone.

David felt warmer. Still bone-cold, but not nearly as icicley as a few seconds ago. He touched his hair. It was cold, but perfectly dry. Except . . . a sore spot on his forehead was wet. He looked at his fingers: blood, not enough to scare him.

He lifted his head and said, "Xander, what did you hit me with?"

"Oh." His brother held up the shiny object David had seen from the water. A sextant, which once helped sailors use the stars to navigate. "This old-fashioned GPS. It was one of the items I picked up to unlock the door. Sorry."

David *thunk*ed his head down. His brain was numb, as though the cold had penetrated and frozen it. He knew, however, that it wasn't the cold that had flipped the off switch in his mind— it was the craziness of what he'd just gone through.

"That wind thing," he said. "It took all the ocean water back where it belonged. Right out of my hair and clothes. How freaky is that?"

"We just survived the sinking of the *Titanic*, and you think the *wind* is freaky?" Xander nudged his cast.

"Among other things," David said. "There's just too many things happening to get my head around them all."

He felt Xander at his side, nodding.

David held up his fist and straightened a finger for each point he made: "We went from Phemus coming after us . . . to Keal fighting him in the clearing . . . to finding out the world gets destroyed sometime in the near future . . . to running from, then running *into*, those future-world humanlike things . . . to nearly freezing to death in the Atlantic—*because we jumped off the* Titanic!" He pushed out a heavy breath. "Did I miss anything?"

Dad patted his leg. He said, "We found Nana. We rescued her."

"Twice," Xander said.

David looked at Dad. "It worked?" he said. "Throwing the creature into the portal instead of Nana worked?"

Dad smiled and nodded. "Next time we have to do something like that, try not to let them pull you in, okay?"

David thought about it, where they had gone. He said, "We killed that guy, that creature."

"Better him than Nana," Xander said.

Dad didn't comment for a while, then: "We didn't know where the portal would take him, Dae. Besides, maybe somebody rescued him."

David tried to imagine that thing jumping into one of the lifeboats, screeching and flying around, scratching and biting people. They'd think he'd gone insane. Probably throw him overboard. He saw Dad watching him and realized Dad didn't think that was the way it had worked out, either.

"So what?" David said. "They find his body and list him as an unidentified victim?"

"*If* they found his body. A lot of people—like twelve hundred—were never found, just lost at sea. A couple hundred were found and never identified."

David blinked at the ceiling. "It's sad," he said.

"Don't worry about it, Dae," Dad said. "He followed us, tried to hurt us."

Then David remembered. He propped himself up on his elbows. "What about Mom? The face, Bob!"

"What about him?" Xander said.

"We saw him. Someone drew him on the ship. It had to be Mom!"

"Back there? On the *Titanic*?" Xander stared at the door as though ready to go back through it.

"Xander," Dad cautioned, "there was nothing we could do. When we got there, it was minutes away from sinking completely. There's nothing we can do now, at least this time."

Xander's mouth was a perfect circle. "What do you mean, this time?"

Dad nodded toward the door. "That world—the *Titanic*—it might come back around. Maybe we'll have another chance."

David felt his brows scrunching together. He said, "What, *before* the sinking? We just saw it go down."

"That's the thing about time travel," Dad said. "It can happen again and again and again. It's just a matter of whether the house opens it up for us again. But you know something? Mom could have been there then, when we were there—in which case, I'm sure she would have gotten on a lifeboat—or she was there some other time and she's in some other world now."

"What if she *was* there," David said. "And she *didn't* get off?"

Dad didn't say anything, and his silence was awful. Finally, he said, "You know, guys, we saw him, Bob. We could just as easily not have seen him. It was a fluke that we did. We were helpless to do anything."

"Don't you want to *know*?" David said. "Don't you *have to*?"

"Of course I want to. As much as you do. But it'd drive us crazy thinking about it, wishing for things that can never be." He looked from David to Xander.

"Like Grandpa," Xander said.

After Dad's mother had been kidnapped into the worlds, his father had spent a couple of months going in and out of the portals looking for her. Eventually, he'd taken the family away, fearing for their safety and his own sanity.

Dad nodded. "I don't know the whole story. Maybe he saw things like that and it got to him. Let's agree that's not going to happen to us, okay?"

Xander turned his gaze back to the portal door. His lips were tight, not liking any of it. Then he said, "Okay."

Dad gave David a sad half smile. "Are you all right? Not going to cry?"

"Give me a minute."

"We need to get you thawed out," Dad said playfully.

David could tell he was making an effort to change the subject, lighten the mood.

"Want a bath?"

"Steaming hot," David said, going along with him. "For three days."

"You'd turn into a raisin," Xander said.

"Better than the Popsicle I feel like now. Toria's okay?"

Xander frowned. "*She* is, yeah."

"What do you mean, *she* is? Xander?"

"Jesse got hurt."

"What?" David said. "How? Is he all right?" His voice was high, and broke on the last word.

"It was bad," Xander said. He brought his heels down from the bench, rose, and sat where his feet had been. "There was lots of blood. Keal took him to the hospital."

"The hospital?" David said. He slid himself out from Xander's head, which clunked down on the floor.

"Hey," Xander said, rubbing the back of his skull.

David got to his feet. "Dad, we have to go."

"I don't think . . ." Dad studied Xander's face. "I don't think there's anything we can do, Dae."

"*Dad!*"

"Let's at least wait until we hear from Keal," Dad said. "See what's up."

David dropped down onto the bench. He covered his face with his hands. What finding himself alone on the deck of the *Titanic* couldn't do, what the icy waters of the black Atlantic couldn't do, what being dunked over and over with barely a breath couldn't do . . . Jesse's injuries did: David began to cry.

Sixteen

WEDNESDAY, 7:39 P.M.

Jesse.

David pictured the old man's face. Skin like a favorite pair of jeans, all wrinkly and worn. Eyes like a gypsy's crystal ball: they saw more than your physical appearance; they seemed to see inside, to your heart. And he had a way of making you feel he liked what he saw. He always said just the right thing to make you feel better. He had offered them hope when they needed it. He was an ally—a friend who truly understood the house and what they were going through. Around Jesse, David felt less lonely, less alone in this mess. Jesse had come to help them . . . and now look.

Dad whispered, obviously to Xander, "Was it Taksidian?"

"Toria thinks so," Xander said. "They saw someone standing in the shadows over Jesse. Then Taksidian went after Nana."

No one spoke. David wept.

After a minute Dad said, "Is that why you came over, after I told you not to?"

"I wanted to help David," his brother answered. His sneakered toe tapped David's hip. "I got to thinking . . . he's been through so much, I couldn't stand *not* helping."

There was silence, and without looking, David knew his dad and his brother were staring at each other.

"Dad," Xander continued, "I'm ready to fall over, and Dae's been through more than I have. I just—"

"Okay, okay," Dad said. "I get it . . . but it almost turned out pretty awful."

Softly, Xander said, "Sorry."

David sniffed. He squeezed his eyes tight, letting the last of his tears roll down his cheeks and pool against the fleshy part of his palms. He said, "Don't you even care about Jesse?"

Dad's fingers clamped over his knee. "Of course we do, Dae. There's just nothing we can do for him right now."

That got David crying again. *Nothing we can do*: that seemed to be the King family slogan these days. Was everything they'd done to make things better—creating the MCC to log and plan their missions; going over time and again searching for Mom; fighting off the cops, Taksidian, Phemus—was everything pointless, like running in place as fast you could? Or did they have to work that hard just to keep from losing ground— without those efforts, would they be way worse off by now? It was a depressing thought. If just surviving took everything they had, drained them like cheap batteries, what would they have to do to actually accomplish anything? How much effort would it take to find Mom? And did they have it to give?

Dad whispered, "Xander, go run David's bath, please."

Xander nudged David with his feet as he pulled them off the bench. Then he squeezed David's shoulder. "It'll be all right, Dae."

The door opened and closed.

Dad let him cry. David knew what he was thinking: that he was overtired, overwhelmed, and overreacting. So he was surprised when Dad sat beside him, put his arm around him, and said, "I like him too, David. I hardly know the old guy, but he feels like he belongs, doesn't he?"

David wiped tears and snot off his face. He rubbed his sloppy hands over his jeans. "He's family."

Dad frowned and nodded. "He's blood. And he's the only other person in the world who understands what's happening here."

David smiled thinly. "He doesn't think we're crazy."

Dad ran his fingers through David's hair. "We're not crazy . . . this house is."

Footsteps pounded in the hallway. The door flew open, and David almost cried out. Toria leaned in.

"What now?" David said. He was teetering on the edge of tears again. He felt worn and thin, like a bicycle tire ready to burst.

Please, Lord, nothing else right now. I need a break.

He realized Toria bore a broad smile, which fell away when her eyes found his face.

"What's the matter, Dae?" She leaned over his knees to hug him.

"*Everything,* Tor." Once it was out, he recognized the truth of it. There were so many big things pressing down on them he didn't even want to list them. It was, as he'd said, *everything.*

"Nana's sleeping," Toria said. "She was just going to 'catch her breath' is what she said, but she's out cold." Toria leaned close to David and whispered, "She snores."

David couldn't help a little smile.

Toria's eyes flashed wide. "Xander said you were on the *Titanic!* Is that true?"

"Yeah, but we didn't see Leonardo DiCaprio."

She punched his shoulder. "I know the difference between a movie and real life."

David rubbed the spot she'd hit. Those hard little fists

hurt. "I'm glad *you* do," he said, "because I don't think I do anymore."

Dad leaned into him. "How about that bath? You'll feel better when you're warm, clean, and rested."

All of that sounded like heaven, but David said, "I doubt it."

"Maybe get some food in you. When was the last time you ate?"

David shook his head. "I can't eat."

Dad stood and guided Toria out the door. "Go see if there's anything in the kitchen. I'll be there in a few minutes. I'll bet we can come up with something David will eat, huh?"

"Oh yeah, I'll bet," she said running off.

"How can she be like that?" David said. "Like everything's okay?"

"Nana's sleeping on her bed," Dad said. "Instead of getting sucked away."

"To the *Titanic*," David said. "That's where she would have gone."

"Right," Dad said. "But she's not there, thanks mostly to you. That's something to be happy about."

"I guess."

"You're tired, Dae. Come on, let's get you feeling better."

CHAPTER

seventeen

WEDNESDAY, 8:09 P.M.

David did feel better. A little. He sat in the bathtub with his knees pulled up to his chest and his arms wrapped around his legs. He rested his chin on one of his knees, watching the bubbles Xander had added to the water slowly dissolve. Steam drifted off the surface, making him feel like he was simmering. That brought to mind a joke Robbie, his best friend from Pasadena, had thought was hilarious: Two cannibals were eating a clown. One said to the other, "Does this taste funny to you?"

David smiled, not at the joke, but at the memory of Robbie. They'd attended different schools but had been on the same soccer team for four years. They'd go to movies, have sleepovers, play practical jokes on Xander and Robbie's sister Cambria. But the best thing was that they'd practiced soccer together at Arroyo Seco Park until they'd become an unstoppable one-two punch as star midfielder and striker. One of them would cross the ball to the other, who would snap it into the goal.

Not only had David not played soccer since coming to Pinedale, but his prospects of ever playing again looked bleak. The middle school didn't even offer it. Besides, who could think of sports when his whole world revolved around rescuing his kidnapped mother and just surviving to see another sunrise? It was a rare treat to simply *think* about something other than the craziness of this house. Since moving in, some danger or another was always challenging him, whether he was in one of the far-off worlds or not.

He blew at the bubbles and watched them break apart. He didn't take many baths these days, but this one hit the spot. When he'd first climbed in, his skin had tingled almost painfully. He'd actually felt the warmth reach his muscles, then his bones. He didn't know how long he'd been sitting there, but he had turned on the hot water twice to keep the water steaming.

The bath reminded him of better times, a long time ago in

Pasadena: Mom was home, his friends were a short walk away, his team had won their last game—or not, it was fun either way. Strange how you didn't really appreciate ordinary things until you didn't have them anymore.

When Dad had announced a few months ago that they were moving to Pinedale so he could take a job as a school principal, David had known their lives would change. He just never could have guessed how drastically different they would become.

David closed his eyes and concentrated on the here and now. Silence. Warmth. Less than an hour ago he had nearly drowned in water so cold that if it weren't salty, it would have been ice. That water had churned, turning the air into a cold, misty spray. By the time he and Dad had plunged into the ocean, most of the ship's lights had gone out, leaving everything black. The sky had a smattering of stars, no moon; the water had appeared dark as oil. Screams and yells had filled the night like the howling of forest animals moving in for a kill.

A noise startled him. He opened his eyes to see Xander slipping into the bathroom. His brother closed the door and pressed his back to it. He wore fresh clothes. His hair was damp and sticking up everywhere. He must have taken a shower in Mom and Dad's bathroom.

David's heart stepped up its pace, the way it had done when Toria had burst into the antechamber. He realized that he was *expecting* the next emergency. That's how constant the onslaught had been.

"What?" he said.

Xander said, "Dad wants us in bed right after dinner."

David relaxed. "Good."

"*Not* good," Xander said. He stepped into the small room, lowered the toilet lid, and sat on it. "We have things to do."

"Like what?"

Xander gaped at him. "Mom?" he said, as if he'd had to remind David of the importance of a beating heart. "We gotta get those walls back up, the ones Phemus knocked down. We have to fortify this place before it all starts up again."

David realized he and Xander were in sync, both of them expecting trouble to come any second. But they were handling it differently. He wanted to enjoy the calm; Xander wanted to use it to prepare for what David had just thought of as the next emergency. He wondered if Xander had any specific trouble in mind. He said, "What starts up again?"

"The attacks. Taksidian, people from other worlds, the cops, like the ones who arrested Dad yesterday . . . who knows what else. You don't think they're going to stop now, do you?"

"Aren't you tired? You told Dad you were ready to fall over."

"I am. But Dae, we'll sleep when we're dead."

The expression startled David. "Where'd you hear that?"

Xander shrugged. "*I'll Sleep When I'm Dead*, pretty cool movie with Clive Owen."

A movie. Of course.

"Well," David said, "that day may come sooner than you

think." He propped his cast on the edge of the tub and dipped his head into the water. He flipped his head back, knowing he was splashing Xander but not caring. He pushed his hair off his face and spat out a stream of water. *Sleep when we're dead.* His brother was losing it.

"It will if we don't take care of business," Xander said. "They know we're weak, Dae. Tired, scared. We're down a man. And Keal's out with him. We're vulnerable, we're . . ."

David returned his head to the water. When he came up, Xander was still talking.

"—been thinking about this. Everything's getting crazier, more—I don't know—*frantic*. I don't think that's just the way it feels."

He paused, and David blinked the water out of his eyes to look at him.

"Something's happening," Xander said. "Or *going* to happen."

"*Something's happening?*" David said. "You just figure that out?"

"No," Xander said, standing. "I mean, something big, bigger than what we've already seen." He squinted at something on the edge of the two, then looked surprised: responding to his own thoughts, David thought. Xander snatched a towel off the rack and dropped to his knees by the tub.

David scowled at him. It was like Xander was breaking into his space, a space he found peaceful and free of all the garbage. Breaking in with worries and his sleep-when-we're-dead attitude. He said, "You're not thinking about using that towel on me, are you? Running the water for me was good enough, thank you."

"Uh . . . no," Xander said. He ran the towel over the edge of the tub.

Before the towel covered it, David thought he saw a smear of red against the white porcelain. "What was that?" he said.

Xander peered under the towel. "Nothing," he said, dropping it to the floor. "Think about it. Taksidian actually hurt Jesse, probably tried to kill him. I think he's tried to kill us, too, like when he came after us through the closet yesterday, and when he sent Phemus and his friends after us. He's not satisfied bribing town officials to get us thrown out anymore. He's *serious*. Deadly serious."

David opened his eyes wide. "No kidding."

"So, why now?" Xander said. "Why all of a sudden? Something's up, I'm telling you."

"Xander, I'm taking a bath."

His brother sat back on the floor. He sighed. "You're not listening."

"I am," David said. "I hear you. You're so tired you're on your second or third wind. You know, so tired you can't sleep, and your mind's going a thousand miles a minute."

"You sound like Dad," Xander said. He twisted his face to make sure David realized it wasn't a compliment.

"Look," David said, "it's not all of a sudden. The house has been throwing stuff at us since we moved in."

"But it's not just about getting Mom back, not now." A drop of water dripped out of Xander's hair and down his face. He swatted at it as though it were a spider. Jumpy. "We've seen the *future*. Everything wiped out. We gotta do something about it, and I think Taksidian knows that. He's going to try to stop us, more than ever. Whatever he's doing that causes what we saw, it has something to do with this house. He needs it. Maybe he's on some kind of timetable. Maybe we've already stopped him from doing something he needs to do. Maybe he's getting desperate."

"That's a lot of maybes," David said. But Xander was probably right. He just didn't want to think about it now.

Xander grabbed the edge of the tub and hoisted himself up. David could tell he wasn't happy.

"The next thing that hits us might force us out of the house for good. Then what are we going to do about Mom?" Xander crossed the room. "Think about it, David. For Mom." He stepped out and closed the door behind him.

David stared at the door. *He's playing me*, he thought. *And he knows the exact buttons to push.* He leaned back against the tub, determined to find the peace his brother had disrupted. But the water had cooled and his heartbeat wasn't slowing and his brother's concerns had invaded his mind.

Aaaahhhh! He slapped the water and yanked on the chain that unplugged the drain.

eighteen

WEDNESDAY, 9:00 P.M.

"Can't we at least go see Jesse?" David said.

Xander, Toria, David, and Dad were sitting around the dining room table, the remnants of grilled cheese sandwiches and tomato soup in front of them. Though Toria had set a plate and bowl out for Nana, their grandmother was still asleep upstairs. Toria had also remembered to put a place setting down for Mom. Dad had told them it was a way of honoring a missing loved one and anticipating her return, but it only made David sad, and Xander even more agitated.

Dad said, "Not tonight, Dae. We'll see how things look in the morning. When Keal called, Jesse was just getting wheeled into the emergency room. We'll have to wait and see."

"But he's going to be all right?"

"He's in good hands, Dae."

David scratched his cast. After his bath, Dad had wrapped an Ace bandage around it to keep it from falling apart. But under all that crumbling plaster, his skin tingled and itched like a thousand mosquito bites.

He pushed a piece of crust across his plate. Despite being sick with worry for Jesse, he had wolfed down more than he thought he could. The whole family had eaten like starving dogs. All that exertion, he guessed, like how hungry he always was after a hard practice.

A knock sounded at the door. They all jumped and looked at each other. David was getting tired of being so jumpy. It was like getting zapped with a cattle prod every time you relaxed.

Dad got up. Xander pushed back from the table, but Dad pointed at him and said, "Wait here." He went into the foyer.

"If it's Taksidian, I'm going to pound him," Xander whispered.

David prayed it wasn't for a million reasons, not the least of which was the image of Taksidian's clawlike fingernails slashing at his brother.

They heard the door open and Dad mumbling something. A deep voice answered.

Dad and Keal walked into the dining room.

David almost jumped up. He said, "How is he? How's Jesse?"

Keal shook his head. "Can't tell you, David. After they rushed him into a treatment room, a nurse started asking questions. You know, who is he, who am I, how'd he get hurt, when'd it happen. I realized that was a can of worms I didn't want to open. None of it would affect the care Jesse got, but it *could* bring a lot of grief down on you guys. You're having enough trouble staying in the house. Last thing you need is an attempted murder here." He looked at Dad. "I assume you're not ready to leave."

"We're not," Dad said. He locked eyes with Xander. "Not till we get Mom back."

"I went to use the bathroom," Keal continued. "When I came out, I slipped away."

"You just *left him?*" David felt like he'd been punched.

"Had to," Keal said.

David thought Keal looked as sad as anyone could look. He knew Keal loved the old man. He wouldn't have left him unless he felt he had no other choice. Still . . . "Shouldn't *someone* be there for him?" David said.

"They're taking care of him," Keal said. "We'll figure out a way to keep tabs on his condition later."

Dad said, "No way they can trace him back to us?"

Keal shook his head. "I didn't give them any information."

Dad patted Keal on the back and headed for his seat. As he passed Nana's setting, he gestured toward it. "Hungry?"

Toria, ever the hostess, said, "That's Nana's, but she's sleeping. You can have it."

Keal dropped into the seat, nodding his thanks. Half of a sandwich disappeared into his mouth.

Xander pushed his plate away, crossed his arms on the table, and dropped his head on them. He said, "I wish we'd never come here."

David couldn't tell if Xander was finally feeling his exhaustion or if he was taking a jab at Dad for bringing them to Pinedale and into the house on purpose. Xander had been furious about it, once Mom had been taken and the King kids had found out that Dad had known about the portals all along. Xander had claimed to be over it, but with everything getting worse and their inability to find Mom as quickly as they'd hoped, David thought it was a wound Xander had opened up again.

Dad said, "Me too, Xander. Me too."

"But then we wouldn't have found Nana!" Toria said.

Xander lifted his head as if to say something, but apparently thought better of it. David could have guessed what was on his brother's mind: *Was finding Nana worth losing Mom? Was it worth risking our own lives time and time again? Was it worth Jesse's injury?*

David closed his eyes. Were these things he thought Xander would think . . . or did he, David, think them? He didn't want to think that way, weighing the value of one person's life over another's. He supposed that was the way of things, though: Parents cared more for their own kids than other people's, even if they were compassionate for everyone. Kids felt the same for their parents. Families—weren't they the ties that bind? Blood thicker than water, and all that. But nothing was that simple. After all, Nana *was* family. So was Jesse.

He said, "Dad, do you know what Jesse meant when he said we were *gatekeepers?*"

Dad squinted at him. "He said that?"

"When we first met him," Xander confirmed. "Right here at this table. You were in jail."

"I don't know," Dad said. "Maybe it has something to do with keeping people like Taksidian from using the portals. Jesse said he thought the destruction we saw in the future world was Taksidian's doing."

"That's why he wants us out of the house," Xander said. "So he can use it."

Dad said, "Like he probably has been doing all these years. He's never lived here. You can tell by what the house looked like when we moved in. It was just the way my father, sister, and I left it thirty years ago."

"Why didn't he just buy it?" Xander said.

Dad shook his head. "Can't. I found out when I inquired

about buying it that the house is deeded to a trust in the family name. Only people in our family tree can live here. I had all the right paperwork to prove who we were."

Keal cleared his throat. He said, "'Course Taksidian could get it condemned so no one could ever live in it. If he could prove it's too dangerous for people."

"It is," David said.

"But for reasons I'm sure he's not going to reveal," Keal said. "Like you, he doesn't want anyone to know about the portals, not if he's planning to use them. He just wants it empty."

"Well," Dad said, "that's not going to happen." He turned to Keal. "Jesse said what we found in the future, the destroyed city—most likely, a destroyed *world*—is Taksidian's doing. Did he tell you anything that would shed some light on that, like *why* Taksidian would do that, or what he's up to that leads to it?"

"Nothing," Keal said. "I can't imagine somebody intentionally wiping out the world."

"Maybe it's *not* intentional," Dad said. "Doesn't matter. What's important is that it does happen. We know it. We saw it. We have to find a way to stop him."

"We need to figure out what he's up to," Xander said.

"How?" David said.

"We turn the tables," Xander said. "We go after *him*."

nineteen

WEDNESDAY, 9:27 P.M.

Yep, David thought, his brother was losing it. Go after Taksidian. Sounded good, in a Bruce Willis or Matt Damon kind of way, but: "How?" David said.

He glanced around the table at the faces all turned toward Xander. It appeared that even Dad and Keal were interested in the answer.

Xander said, "Find out where he lives, what he does for a

living, what other things he is up to—besides terrorizing us, I mean. Maybe we'll find something that will put the pressure on *him* for a change, get him to back off."

"Or come at us with an army or something," David said.

"Like he hasn't already? Come on, there's gotta be something. Dad, you know, the best defense is a good offense, right?"

"Well . . ." Dad said, thinking.

Keal nodded. "He does seem to be coming at you with guns blazing. Wouldn't hurt to try to find something to throw back at him."

"Like a hand grenade," David said. "You don't happen to have one, do you?"

Keal smiled. "Figuratively, maybe we can find one, if we can dig up some dirt on the guy." He eyed Xander. "And Xander, for you the operative word in that sentence is *figuratively*. Don't go trying to get your hands on any weapons."

Xander's face said that he was either insulted that Keal felt the need to tell him that or disappointed that real bombs weren't involved in the plan.

"Wait a minute," David said. "You're the guy who led us right *into* those creatures today. Of course you're going to say, 'Let's charge Taksidian.' That's what you'd do."

Keal shrugged. "It worked," he said.

"Barely," David said weakly. It was hard to argue with success.

"'Barely' is the difference between sitting at this table now . . . and not," Keal said.

"Okay, then," Xander said. "Let's do it."

"Do what?" Toria said.

For a moment Xander looked as perplexed as Toria did. Then he said, "Computers. We can tap into all kinds of databases. Like the movie *War Games* . . . or *Eagle Eye*. I bet we can find out the brand of his underwear!" He looked around the table and offered a little shrug. "If we wanted to."

"That's how it's done," Keal said, nodding. "One puzzle piece at a time. Before you know it, you have something you can act on. Sometimes."

"We can ask around too," Xander continued, his eyes wide with excitement. "See what people know. And, and . . . why not confront him? We can go to him and—"

"Whoa, whoa," Keal said, holding his hand up. "We have to remember this is one bad dude." He grabbed his index finger. "Anyone who—" He stopped, looked around, lowered his hands.

"What?" David said. He knew there was something more, something Keal wasn't saying.

"Nothing." Keal looked down at his plate.

Dad reached across the table and touched his arm. "Keal, if there's something else . . . I think we need to know everything."

"He . . ." Keal said. "He took one of Jesse's fingers."

Toria gasped and covered her mouth.

"His *finger?*" David said. "Jesse's finger?" The image in his head wasn't of a missing finger, it was of a finger being cut off. The snap of the bone, the . . . Like Toria, he covered his mouth, but in his case it was to help him keep his sandwich down.

Keal nodded. "It's bad enough that Taksidian stabbed him. There's something . . . I don't know . . . more gruesome about taking the man's finger."

"I thought there was something wrong with his hand when I lifted it," Xander said. "But then I saw the blood and figured that was it, just a lot of blood."

They looked at each other, all of them apparently at a loss for words. When David felt that he had his stomach under control, he said, "Why would he do that?"

Keal frowned. "When murderers do it, it's called taking a trophy. It reminds them of their deed."

"That's *sick,*" Toria said.

"It goes beyond murder," Keal agreed. "It indicates a sort of bloodlust, something the killer does, not out of some perceived need but because he likes it."

"We can't stay," Dad pronounced. "Not with someone like that after us."

"We're not leaving," Xander said. "You promised, and you just said it again, not five minutes ago."

"Xander—"

"No! You said until we find Mom!"

Dad sighed. "That was when we had only the portals and the people who came out of them to worry about. It's different now."

"No!" Xander said again. "I knew this would happen. I knew you'd changed your mind! Just like Grandpa Hank did!"

"I don't want to leave, Xander," Dad said, "but surely you can see that it's too dangerous to stay. I just——" He shook his head. He looked like horses were pulling him in different directions.

David was glad it was a decision *he* didn't have to make: run from a cold-blooded madman and leave Mom, or stay and hope they could keep Taksidian from killing them.

Keal cleared his throat. He touched a napkin to his lips. He said, "I know it isn't my place to say anything, but . . ." He looked Dad square in the eyes, his face conveying sympathy, even shared pain. "You *can't* leave," he said. "You can't. Not without your wife." He took a deep breath. "And not after seeing the future."

Dad started to protest, and Keal patted the air between them in a calming gesture. "I know, I know. But maybe we *can* find Mrs. King and fight off Taksidian at the same time."

"And save the world," Xander said.

Keal looked at him. Something passed between them that bent their lips into smiles. Keal let out a short laugh. "Sounds crazy, doesn't it?"

He swung his smile toward David, and David couldn't help but smile back.

"What's crazy is smiling about it," David said.

"Absolutely," Keal said, showing all his teeth. He lowered and raised his head in an exaggerated nod. "My mama used to say, when you don't know whether to laugh or cry, laugh. I don't know why it is we're here, in this impossible situation, but I do believe we can make *anything* better." He turned back to Dad. "If we try."

Xander slapped David on the back. He said, "That's your cue, Dae."

David smiled and said, "Let's do it."

twenty

David knew his father's heart. If there were any way they could stay, they would. Dad looked at Keal a long time, then at each of them in turn. He stopped on Xander and said, "All right. We stay. But we're going to have to fortify this place."

Xander said, "Locks everywhere. Cameras. An alarm system. Whatever it takes."

"And a plan to get the job done," Keal said. He held up his

index finger. "We have to keep Taksidian at bay. Maybe we can find out something about him that'll help." A second finger went up. "We have to find your mother." Finger number three: "We have to do something about the future."

"What can we do?" David said. Keal might as well have told them they had to flap their arms and fly to the moon. But then, David thought, everything he thought he'd known about the world, about what was possible and what wasn't, had pretty much gone out the window when they'd moved into the house. So far they'd teleported from a linen closet to a school locker miles away in a matter of seconds; they'd flown through the air and hovered forty feet above the ground; they'd fought gladiators and the German army; they'd traveled back in time and saved a little girl who in turn saved the world from smallpox. Keal's list of tasks *did* sound crazy, but possible, doable.

"One piece of the puzzle at a time," Keal reminded him. "You got yourself a pretty cool command center upstairs."

"Mission Control Center," Toria corrected.

"The MCC. Right," said Keal. "Let's start using it, *really* using it. We'll gather everything we know about this house, the portals, Taksidian. Maybe something will pop out at us."

"I hope it's not Phemus," David said.

Keal pointed at him. "Phemus . . . he's another problem we gotta figure out. How do we keep him from coming into the house?"

Okay, David thought. *Anything else? An earthquake? The ground opening up and swallowing us? The plague?*

He didn't say any of that, though. Instead he told Keal, "We already tried putting locks on the doors. The house tore them off."

Keal squinted at him, nodded. "Good to know," he said. "Let's gather everything together and make a plan."

"Nana," Xander said. "She was on the other side—I guess that's what you'd call it—for thirty years. She told Toria that she moved from one world to another. She's gotta know a lot. We need to debrief her."

"Do *what* to her?" Toria said.

"Talk to her," Xander said. "Find out what she knows."

"I'll bet Jesse knows more," David said. "But he's . . ." He let a frown finish for him.

Xander seemed to remember something. He leaned over the table toward Keal. "Did you see the symbols Jesse wrote?"

"The what?"

"Hold on." Xander hopped up, ran out of the room, and clambered up the stairs.

"Symbols?" Keal asked Dad, who shook his head.

A few moments later, Xander darted into the room. He slapped a pad of notebook paper on the table. "Okay, look," he said. "Jesse wants us to do something. He wrote these symbols on the floor."

"On the floor?" David said. "How—"

Xander's look made him stop. *Oh*, he thought.

They leaned in.

"What are they?" Toria asked.

"A house," David said, pointing. "Is that an umbrella?"

"I thought maybe an ax," Xander said.

"What's that?" Toria said, tapping her finger on the third symbol, which could have been buck teeth or, if turned upside down, two buildings on a hill.

"Antechamber items," Dad said. "He wants us to find a portal."

twenty-one

WEDNESDAY, 9:39 P.M.

"Yeah," Xander said. "Three items, that's what it takes to open the portal. But I don't remember seeing these things."

Dad tilted his head. "They're always changing, the antechambers, the worlds they lead to. I don't think we've seen half of them, or even a tenth."

David sat back. "But why a portal?"

"Guess we'll know when we find it," Dad said.

"Do you think it has something to do with Mom?" David asked, trying not to get his hopes up.

"Everything about this house has something to do with rescuing Mom," Dad said. "That's why we're here."

"Wherever it leads to, it must be important," Xander said. "A place that will help us."

David blew out through his lips. "That'd be a nice change." But he knew Xander was right. Jesse—despite vowing never to return to the house, despite being ninety-something years old, despite his wheelchair—had come all the way from Chicago to help them. He would have spent his last breath trying to do that.

"Well," Xander said. He slapped his palms on the table and stood. "What are we waiting for?"

"Now?" David said. "You want to find the portal *now*?"

"Why not?" Xander said.

"It's late. I'm beat. Do you remember the kind of day we had?"

"Hey, we'll sleep—"

"Stop!" David said. "Don't you say we'll sleep when we're dead." He gaped at his father. "He's been saying that. He wants to just keep going till we all fall over."

"Xander," Dad said. "David has a point. We need—"

"We *need* to get stuff done," Xander interrupted. "The portal, the MCC, fortification, Nana—"

"Xander," Keal said. He was calm, but his rumbling voice commanded attention.

All faces—including Xander's—turned to him.

Keal continued: "Not tonight." He leveled a firm finger at Xander. "You're exhausted, I can tell. You have to get some sleep. We all do." He lowered his finger and his eyes. Then he addressed Dad. "I'm sorry. I shouldn't talk to your boy like that."

"No," Dad said. "Go ahead."

David nodded. Keal was in the Special Forces, a military man. What they were saying—about using the MCC, going on the offensive—it was military talk. Keal was exactly what they needed.

Keal pinched the bridge of his nose between his eyes, then rubbed his close-cropped hair. "Here's the deal, Xander. You've had a long, crazy day. Enough action to knock a soldier off his feet. And—"

"Keal—" Xander started.

Keal stopped him with a word: "*And.*" He focused intense eyes on Xander until he was sure the boy was listening. "And I know you guys were up late last night. Jesse and I didn't leave here until after two in the morning. You gotta be running on fumes. Don't say you aren't."

He leaned back in the chair. "I learned something about this in officer candidate school. How much sleep soldiers need is a part of wartime strategy. Sleep deprivation happens to soldiers and whole armies. They just keep fighting on, especially if it seems either victory or defeat is imminent."

Keal touched his fingers to his head. "What happens is this. The mind gets so exhausted, it wants to shut down. After a while, the brain gives up asking for rest. It *pretends* to kick into gear again, just to keep up with the body. But sleep deprivation impairs alertness, cognitive performance, and mood. It causes paranoia, hallucinations, faulty thinking. General Patton said, essentially, the idea is not to give up sleep for your country, but to make the other poor guy give up sleep for his." He paused to give Xander that piercing glare again. "Xander, we need you at your best. You need to sleep. We all do."

Xander blinked slowly, then dropped down in his chair. He said, "For how long?"

"A *good* sleep," Keal said. "I *insist*." He looked at Dad, who nodded.

Xander seemed to frown with his whole face. He scowled at David.

"Don't think of sleep as downtime," Keal said. "It's part of the battle, as important as planning and action."

"Fine," Xander said, rising again. "Let's get it over with."

CHAPTER

twenty-two

WEDNESDAY, 10:10 P.M.

In the foyer, David gave his grandmother a hug. He backed away and glanced at Dad, who stood in the open doorway, waiting to take her to a motel in town.

She'd gotten up shortly after Xander had stormed off to their bedroom; it was probably his angry clomping that had awakened her. Dad, Keal, and Nana had talked it out and decided she was better off out of the house.

To Nana, David said, "Are you sure you want to go?"

She touched her fingers to his face. "I'd rather not leave you, David. We have a lot of catching up to do." She looked up toward the second floor. "It's this house that doesn't want me here. Or I should say, it wants me too badly. It'll be safer for everyone if I don't spend too much time here."

David turned to Dad. "But I thought . . . you know, the creature . . ."

"We can't be sure that was a permanent fix," Dad said.

"Will she be safe away from us?" David said. He looked at Toria, who was standing behind Nana, gripping a handful of their grandmother's skirt. His sister's eyes were red, and tears still glimmered on her cheeks. "You said Toria can't go because she'd be safer here."

"And I think Nana would be as well, with all of us watching out for each other," Dad said. "Except for the pull. It wants Nana, not Toria. Any dangers out there can't be as great as the one here. At least for Nana."

"What about Taksidian?" David said.

"We'll make sure no one's following us. We'll slip her into the room Keal and Jesse already have, so we won't have to check in anywhere."

"And I have my dinner," Nana said, holding up Toria's pink *High School Musical* lunchbox. She smiled back at his sister. "Thank you, Toria."

"Why can't Keal stay with you?" Toria said.

Nana's eyes found Keal sitting on the stairs. "I'd feel better if he were here with you. Don't worry, I'll be fine. I'll see you tomorrow." She returned her gaze to David. "Then we'll see if I can shed any light on those worlds to help you find your mom. You'll tell Xander that for me, won't you?"

David smiled. "He can debrief you then."

She gave him another quick squeeze and Toria a longer one. She and Dad left, and David locked the door behind them. He turned to see Keal pointing at him.

"Bed," Keal said. He swung his finger to Toria. "You too."

CHAPTER

twenty-three

WEDNESDAY, 10:52 P.M.

David rolled over, scrunching the pillow into a ball under his head. Moonlight coming in the window caught the edges of Xander's dark figure. He was sitting up in bed.

"Go to sleep," David groaned.

Instead, Xander swung his legs off the bed. "This sucks."

"You heard what Keal said. You need to sleep."

Xander made a rude noise with his lips. "He doesn't know me."

"Sounds like he knows a lot," David said. He lifted his head, propped an arm under it. "I've been thinking."

"Uh-oh."

"What do you think of Keal?" David asked.

"He's cool."

"He's more than that," David said. "He's strong. He was an Army Ranger, so he knows weapons, combat, strategy, tactics."

"He's a *nurse* now," Xander said, as though that somehow made Keal less of a tough guy.

David didn't think so. He said, "Right. Look at what's happened to us. We've been beat up, cut up, pounded on, bashed."

"So?"

"So, he's exactly what we need. He has all the skills we can use, from fighting to getting patched up. Don't you think that's strange?"

"Strange how?" Xander swung his legs around to sit on the edge of his bed.

"Dad always says coincidence is baloney."

"What are you saying?" Xander asked. "That *God* sent Keal to us?"

"*Exactly* the guy we need right now?" David said. "If that's not God, what is?"

Xander didn't say anything.

David continued. "Remember that verse Mom used to quote when things got tough? Not *this* kind of tough, but like when she backed into that car and the guy pretended he had whiplash and said he was going to sue? She always said, 'If God is for you, who can be against you?'"

"Uh, let's see: Taksidian? Phemus? This house?"

"It doesn't mean people aren't going to *try* to get you," David said. "It means they won't win."

"They're doing a pretty good job," said Xander.

"But they haven't won. Somehow we've always gotten away. We're still in the house. We still have a chance. Now, of all the people in the world, Keal shows up."

"Hey," Xander said, a little too enthusiastically, "maybe he's an angel. Like *you!*"

"I'm not saying that. But it can't be a coincidence that who we needed is who showed up."

"We needed someone to rescue Mom and get us out of this place," Xander said.

"Maybe that's what's happening. He's helping us do that."

"I meant like *that.*" Xander snapped his fingers. "Oh, never mind. If God is for us, why did Mom get kidnapped in the first place?"

David had thought about that and hadn't come up with an answer. So he said something else he had heard. "Sometimes bad things happen to good people."

Xander's silhouette threw up its arms. "Oh, well . . . which is it, then: is God for us, or is He allowing bad things to happen to good people?"

"I don't know," David said. "Mom said sometimes things

that look bad are really good. We just can't see it when we're in the middle of it." He expected Xander to cut that down with a snide comment too. When he didn't, David said, "Well, I think someone up there is helping us."

"I hope you're right," Xander whispered. They were silent for a while. Then Xander said, "We never finished putting up the camera."

"You want to do that now?" David said. "*Up there?*"

Xander thought about it. "Maybe not that, but something."

"Remember how we used to talk at night? I liked that."

"We talked about this house, before we moved in. I thought it was haunted."

"Guess you were right," David said. "Not by ghosts, though. What was it Jesse said, something about Time haunting this place?"

Xander's dark form nodded. He said, "We thought this room was spooky." He laughed. "Little did we know, huh?"

"It's still kinda spooky," David said. "I keep thinking something else is going to happen, and I don't have any idea where it'll come from. Look at the linen closet, the way it's a different kind of portal—to our school, of all places. And it's down here on the second floor, right outside our bedroom door. Just goes to show, weird stuff can happen anywhere in this house."

Okay, he'd just scared himself. He suddenly had the feeling something was watching them from a dark corner of the room. He rolled onto his back, lifted his head, and looked into the shadows by the closet. He scanned around to the corner where the room opened up to the octagon-shaped area in the house's tower. It was in front of that area's center window that Dad had been waiting to scare them when they first moved in. David had almost peed his pants.

Xander said, "You know, as much as we've learned about this house, there's so much more we don't know."

David sat up and scooted back to lean against the headboard: all the better to keep his eye on the entire room. He said, "Like what?"

"Like *why*," Xander said. "Why is it here?"

"Jesse built it."

"I mean, why does it do what it does? What are the portals all about? And that's just for starters. What's Taksidian doing with them? Why was Mom taken?"

White light flared up against Xander, revealing him sitting there in pajama bottoms and a T-shirt. David's breath stopped in his throat. Then Xander swiveled his head toward the window, and David realized that the light was shining through.

Xander stood and leaned over the nightstand. He pushed aside the thin sheers that covered the window and said, "Dad's home." The light went off, and he sat again. "I'm glad Nana's out. It's better for her."

"Maybe we should all go," David said. He lifted a glass of water off the nightstand and downed half of it.

"We can't risk leaving the house empty," Xander said. "You know that. Taksidian might do something that keeps us out for good. Then we'd never find Mom."

They heard the door open, then shut, downstairs. It was more of a shudder that came up through the floor than a sound.

David finished the water and set it down. He said, "You really think we can find out something about him, about Taksidian? Something that'll help?"

"That's it," Xander said. "I can look him up on the Internet."

"We're not connected yet," David reminded him. Their Mac hadn't come with a modem. They had a broadband modem, but they hadn't ordered the service yet. A lot of things had fallen through the cracks after Mom got taken.

"The school is," Xander said.

"The . . . You're talking about going through the linen closet? No, Xander. We promised Dad no more sneaking around. Besides, Taksidian might expect us to do something like that. He's probably waiting for us at the school."

"He's just a guy, Dae. He can't be everywhere at once."

They heard Dad's footsteps in the hall. The sound faded as he entered his bedroom.

Xander stood.

"He has people working for him," David reminded him. "The watchers."

"If he's all-knowing, all-seeing, he'd have gotten to us by now." He started for the door.

"Xander, wait! Do it tomorrow."

"Dad says we have to go to school," Xander said. "Got to keep up appearances, you know? I don't have computer class, and I won't be able to get to a computer without people around. Now or never, Dae. Want to come?"

David crossed his arms over his chest. "No."

Xander reached the door. "You sure?"

"I'll tell Dad."

"No, you won't." He turned the handle, cracked the door. A thin line of light sliced the darkness.

"Wait!" David said. He hopped up out of bed. He was halfway across the room when Xander swung open the door. David squinted against the hallway light, which Dad had left on, and stopped dead in his tracks.

Keal was sitting in the chair they had propped against the linen closet door. A magazine rested in his lap. He said, "Boys."

Xander gaped at him. "What are you doing?"

Keal flashed a wide grin. "Making sure you get your sleep."

Xander swung a stunned gaze at David, who said, "The sleep police."

Xander turned back to Keal. "You gotta be kidding."

"Good night, guys," Keal said.

Xander shut the door. "This sucks," he said.

twenty-four

THURSDAY, 1:23 A.M.

David's bladder woke him. He considered sleeping through his need but decided he couldn't. Groggily, he flipped back his blankets and sat up. Everything ached: his broken arm, his forehead where Xander had conked him with the sextant, the top of his skull where the wall had landed when Phemus pushed it down, his cheek where Phemus had punched it, his palm where he had grabbed Phemus's obsidian blade, his shoulder where the warrior's arrow had nicked it in the jungle world, and all of his muscles . . . just because they did. If they stayed in the house much longer, he'd end up one big walking wound.

In the next bed, Xander snored in a slow, steady rhythm.

So much for all that stuff Xander said about not getting a wink of sleep, no way, no how, David thought.

And if Xander hadn't yapped about going through the linen closet/locker portal to use the school's computers, David wouldn't have drunk the water, and he wouldn't be up now.

Thanks, Xander.

Groaning as quietly as possible, David stood. He stumbled to the door and opened it. The hall light was blazing. He shielded his eyes with his hand. Keal was still in the chair. David thought he was staring down at the magazine in his lap, then he realized the man was asleep.

David stepped into the hall. A floorboard creaked.

"Whoa! Hey!" Keal said, his head snapping up. He brought up the magazine as if it were a weapon. His eyes focused on David. "What—?"

"Potty break," David said. He walked past Keal and into the bathroom.

Washing his hands, he looked at the boy staring out at him from the mirror. Not the self he knew and loved. This one was almost as pale as the creatures they had seen in the future world. He had dark circles under his eyes. The left side was darker and bigger than the right; it was a true black eye, not just tired. Below it, his cheek was still discolored: red, yellow, blue. The hair on one side rose straight up. He thought, *Poor kid, whoever you are.* He leaned close. Same hazel eyes. At least that part of him was unchanged.

He switched off the light and went into the hall. Keal's chin was touching his chest again.

Something clanged in the other direction. He looked. The far end of the hallway was dark. The lights in the corridor leading to the third-floor stairwell had shorted out when the walls collapsed. The ceiling down there creaked. A door banged.

David swung his head around, sure that the sound would have awakened Keal. But no, the man hadn't budged.

Wake him, he thought.

Just a sec.

In this house, if everyone got up whenever there was a noise, no one would sleep. Ever.

He stood without moving just outside of the bathroom. The toilet was gurgling softly. He strained his ears to hear past it.

Something bumped. Definitely. Too quietly to be on this floor. Had to be upstairs.

Okay . . . so? Last night someone or something had thumped around up there for half the night. That's why Xander had wanted to install the camera. Whatever had made the noise hadn't ventured into the main part of the house. David didn't think so, anyway. They hadn't opened the master bedroom door, where he, Xander, and Toria were bedded down. But last night two walls had separated the third floor from the second. Tonight the walls were gone. Would the thing upstairs take that as an invitation to come down?

David shook his head. He didn't even know if it *was* a "thing." It could be nothing more than the doors up there opening and shutting. They'd witnessed that before, when the doors ripped off the locks he and Dad had put on them.

The camera. Xander hadn't finished mounting it, but it was there, above the doorway between the hallway and the landing. David had seen Xander tightening the screws when Phemus and his cohorts had come up behind him. If he could get to the MCC, he could take a peek at the monitor.

But the MCC was so close to the stairs, the collapsed walls nearly reached its door. Did he dare get that close?

He started walking. Slowly. On his toes. He let his arm brush the wall as he moved toward the end of the hall.

He looked back at Keal. Why not wake him?

Because I'm not a baby. I'm strong and courageous. Strong and courageous. Could you say you were brave if you never acted bravely?

He took another step, then another. He was in front of Toria's open door now. Her night-light filled the room with a faint yellow glow. Her little body barely lifted the blankets off the mattress.

As he passed the banister, he glanced at the chandelier that hung over the foyer. He remembered the way it had thrown glowing diamonds on the walls when he and Xander had cast their flashlights on it. That was when they had first seen Phemus, standing at the end of hall, watching them.

His stomach clenched up. The end of the hall wasn't *completely* dark. Light from the overheads showed him the far wall. If someone were standing there now, he'd see him. But if someone were standing just around the corner . . .

Strong and courageous.

He kept moving. Nearing Dad's room. Almost to the end.

This was when people in a movie audience would say, *Don't go there, stupid!*

Dad's door was open. His father's breathing was slow and deep.

Something rattled. David didn't think it came from the bedroom.

He whispered, "Dad?"

Nothing.

Opportunity number two to get help, David thought. *Just say his name louder. Do it.*

He walked past.

He had a thought: you could never trust noises in this house. What if the sounds he'd heard weren't coming from upstairs? What if someone was creeping up the main staircase? Or sneaking up behind him?

He spun around so fast, his cast banged the wall. Keal's head came up. It slumped down again. No one else in the hall.

He could see a bit of the main stairs. No one was looking at him from there.

He thought he heard Dad mumble. Then the steady breathing resumed.

Three distinctive sounds reached him: *thump-thump-thump.* Footsteps. He was sure they'd come from upstairs.

If they were upstairs, then they weren't down here. He hurried to the corner and peered around it. It was darkest where the walls used to be, farthest from the glow of the main hallway lights. The bottom of the stairs, the only part he would have been able to see, was also pitch-black. But he could make out the edge of one of the steps, maybe the third one from the bottom. The scantest of light was spilling down from the third-floor hallway.

He tiptoed diagonally across the hall toward the MCC's door. More stairs came into view, each one better lighted as they progressed toward the landing. He slipped into the room. The desk on which the monitor rested was six or eight feet in. He reached it and switched on the monitor.

Come on, come on.

The footsteps again. Soft, stealthy.

The monitor glowed a solid blue. The wireless camera receiver was off. He grabbed the little box and punched the switch. Snowlike static rolled on the screen. When the snow cleared, a face stared out from the monitor at David.

CHAPTER

twenty-five

THURSDAY, 1:30 A.M.

David jumped. Then he recognized the face and relaxed. It was the wall lamp that depicted a scowling Mongolian-looking warrior. The camera must have been canted toward it; the face appeared to be tilting its head curiously.

Then a blur flashed across the screen, moving left to right: something had passed the camera, heading for the landing!

He backed toward the door. He wanted to turn and run,

but he couldn't tear his eyes off the monitor. Nothing else moved on the screen.

He was at the door. He leaned his head close to the jamb, listening.

Thump.

On the landing.

Thump-thump.

Something was coming down the stairs.

David held his breath. No way he could get out of the room now without being seen. He considered his options: Hide in the MCC. Yell for Dad and Keal. Run for the bedrooms like a man on fire for a lake. He liked that one.

He bolted out of the room, eyes on the target: the corner where the small corridor made a ninety-degree turn into the second floor's main hallway.

His foot caught on a piece of the fallen wall, and he went down. He belly flopped on the floor, knocking the wind out of him and cracking his chin and his cast.

Thump—the footstep. *Creak*—on the steps. Close, maybe six steps up.

David tried to scream, but the air had whooshed out of him and he was fighting to get it back. The only sound he made was a feeble *hhhaaa-hhhaaa-hhhaaa*, like an old smoker trying to laugh. He rolled onto his side to better see the terror descending the stairs.

Legs, stepping down, one stair at a time. The light on the

stairs came from behind David's attacker, which cast the legs in shadow. They seemed spindly, spiderlike.

It was close now, stepping off the bottom stair, in the darkest part of the corridor. A few more steps and it would catch the glow of the main hallway light. David would take to the grave the image of his killer.

He had delayed too long; the beast was *right there*. If he tried to scramble away, it would be on him in seconds. Instead he dove *toward* the creature, to the fallen walls. He swept his hands around over the gritty, plaster-dust-covered slabs. His fingers wrapped around the very thing he had hoped to find: a broken wood stud. He hefted it up. It was three or three and a half feet long. He rose to his knees and jabbed at his attacker.

The beast let out a high-pitched chirp of a scream.

David's arms halted in the process of pistoning back to ram the stud forward again.

He leaned forward. The beast was still cloaked in shadow, but he noticed it was much smaller than the other people who had emerged from the portals. That, along with the voice he had recognized, made him say, "Toria?"

"David?" She stepped into the dim light. She wore her favorite frilly nightgown and nothing on her feet. Her eyes were wide with fear. Her bottom lip trembled.

David tossed the stud aside. He walked on his knees to her and grabbed her shoulders. "What were you doing up there?" He lifted his gaze to take in the staircase, the landing at the top, the light spilling in from the hallway. "Is something up there?"

"I . . . don't . . . know," she said. Little hitches of breath separated her words; she was trying not to cry. "You . . . scared . . . me."

"*I* scared *you*? Are you kidding? I thought . . ." He was disappointed in himself for assuming the lump of blankets on Toria's bed was her. Probably, if he looked now, he'd wonder how he could have thought she was there. *The mind sees what it expects to see*, he thought. He said, "What were you doing up there?"

She swallowed, got her breathing under control. "I thought I heard Mom, David. She was calling me."

"Calling you?" David said. A chill tickled the back of his neck. "Are you sure it was Mom?"

"I think so."

The thought of it—of Toria hearing a voice floating to her from upstairs—scared him so much he thought he was going to be sick. He said, "So you just went? You can't do that." He gazed again toward the landing. "What happened? What'd you find?"

"Nothing," she said. "I turned on the lights up there and looked around, but I didn't find Mom. I started looking in the little rooms, the antechambers, but I got scared. When I was at the top"—she pointed to the top of the stairs—"I saw you, but I wasn't sure it was you. I was trying to get a closer look, without you seeing me. You know, in case you weren't you."

David scanned his sister's face. She was only three years younger, and she was pretty smart for her age, thanks to her love of reading, but he'd always thought of her as a *lot* younger, a baby. Maybe it was because she *was* the baby of the family, and Mom and Dad sort of doted on her that way, or maybe it was because she was a girl. It scared him silly that she'd wandered up to the third floor by herself—whether or not someone had coaxed her, which he didn't want to think about.

He turned aside to listen for movements in the hallway. How could Keal and Dad not have heard Toria's scream or the stud he'd tossed down? He hoped it was because those noises weren't as loud as they had seemed to him, or that the two adults were deep in sleep. He didn't want the house to be messing with the noises: one, it was creepy, and two, it might signal trouble.

"We have to tell Dad about this," David told his sister. "You know that, right?"

She nodded.

"Okay, let's . . ."

A voice stopped him. It was their mom's, drifting down the stairwell to them: "Toria . . . Toria . . ."

CHAPTER

twenty-six

Thursday, 1:34 a.m.

"See?" Toria said. "Doesn't that sound like—"

David clamped his hand over her mouth. "Shhhh." He squatted, pulling his sister down with him. He kept his eyes on the upstairs landing. He expected shadows to flicker through the light, as whoever was up there moved closer. He stared without blinking for so long, his eyes began to burn. Little dots started to float in from the sides.

He blinked, flicked his gaze toward Toria. Watching his reaction, she seemed more frightened by him than by what might be calling her name.

He whispered, "Mom wouldn't just call your name. She'd come running. She'd be screaming to get back to us." He felt Toria's lips moving against his palm. He continued, "I'm going to take my hand away. Be quiet."

She nodded. When she could, she said, "If it's not Mom, who is it?"

David listened. No noises at all: no movements, no more calling. "I don't know."

"What do we do?"

He knew Xander would charge upstairs, opening doors, swinging a bat at shadows; eventually, he'd wind up in another world.

David wasn't Xander. He stood, grabbed Toria's hand. "Come on."

Five minutes later, David, Toria, Dad, and Keal stood on the fallen wall. Dad had made what he called an executive decision to let Xander sleep. They started up the flight of steps, listening.

After a few minutes, Toria said, "But I heard it. I did."

David nodded. "I did too."

"Could it have been someone sounding like your mom?" Keal said. "You know, to lure you up there."

David shrugged. The voice hadn't been that clear, and it'd

spoken only a three-syllable word, twice. *To-ri-a . . . To-ri-a.* "It was pretty creepy," he said.

"So it wasn't Mom," Dad said.

"Only because I knew it couldn't be," David said. "She wouldn't do that. But it sounded like her."

Toria looked up at Keal as if into a tall tree. "I did go up there, and nothing happened to me. If someone wanted to get me up there, why didn't anything happen?"

"Maybe they heard *me*," David suggested. "I might have scared them away."

"All we can do is check it out," Dad said.

Then he did something that startled David. Instead of creeping up the stairs, some club held high, trying not to make the boards creak, he turned and went up fast, two at a time. Keal went right behind him. David realized that Dad's approach wasn't so bad. It was faster, less scary, and didn't expose them to dangers any more than going up more sneakily would have. He grabbed his sister's hand and followed.

The hallway was just as they had left it. All the doors were closed. The aluminum ladder leaned against the far wall. A couple of wall lights were broken or on the floor, the result of various battles. David saw that Xander's camera was as he suspected: twisted to view not the crooked hallway, but the Mongolian-faced wall lamp.

Dad opened an antechamber door, peered in, closed it. He

went to the next door and repeated the process. Keal started up on the other side of the room.

"What are you looking for?" David said.

"We'll know it when we see it," Dad said.

Something about their attitudes heartened David. They acted as though they *belonged* here. This was their house, and they wouldn't be scared into acting like wimps. He strode to a door farther along the hallway, grabbed the handle, and froze. All the fear he'd felt in the second-floor hallway came rushing back. That eerie Mom-voice kept echoing around his skull.

That wasn't Mom, he thought. *No way. And if it wasn't, then what was it?*

The way things were going, he wouldn't be surprised to find some wicked dude lurking behind a door. Well, that wasn't quite right: he'd be surprised out of his socks.

Strong and . . .

Oh, get on with it, will you?

He yanked the door open. Nothing unusual—as far as antechambers went. A white leather jacket with patches of company logos stitched onto the arms, a fire extinguisher, a free-standing speedometer or tachometer or some other ome-ter. He went to the next one. This time he didn't hesitate . . . much. The items behind the door made him smile: a rubber clown nose, big floppy shoes, a high-wire balancing pole, a lion trainer's whip. He wasn't a big fan of circuses—something about the clowns gave him the creeps—but as long as he was on *this* side of the portal, it seemed funny that one of the destinations was Carnival World.

Step right up, folks! See the kid who can change history! Watch him dodge Civil War bullets, Ming Dynasty arrows, and World War II bombs!

David shut the door and moved on.

He pushed open the next door. He kept hold of the handle, leaning into the room, ready to pull the door shut again. What he saw on the floor made him lose his grip.

He fell, and came down nose to nose with Toria's talking teddy bear, Wuzzy. Its half-bead eyes stared at him. Then it spoke to him in Mom's voice: "Toria . . . Toria . . ."

twenty-seven

THURSDAY, 1:59 A.M.

"With everything going on, I forgot about Wuzzy," David said.

He was sitting next to Toria on the antechamber bench. Dad stood against the opposite wall, and Keal leaned his shoulder against the doorjamb. They were all staring down at the teddy bear on the floor as though it were a snippy little dog who liked to bite.

"What *is* it?" Keal said.

"My friend," Toria said, pouty. She looked betrayed by the stuffed animal, and David supposed in a way she had been; scaring them like that certainly wasn't very friendly.

"It has a memory chip in it," David said. "It records what it hears and plays it back."

He remembered the drive up from Pasadena to Pinedale. Toria had driven Xander crazy by making Wuzzy mimic his words in a continuous loop: "Nothing but trees," Xander had complained, looking out the window as they neared town. "Nothing but trees."

"And it's playing back your mom's voice?" Keal said.

David nodded. "That was her. Definitely."

"What's he *doing* up here?" Toria said.

"I think someone wanted to get you alone," David said.

"David," Dad said. His tone said he didn't want David scaring Toria.

"Someone did," David said. He *did* want to scare her. "And it worked. She came up here, Dad. Maybe she didn't go far enough down the hallway to get grabbed, or my noises downstairs kept them from doing it, but they *could have* gotten her!"

Dad frowned at David, but his expression softened.

He knows I'm right, David thought.

Dad turned worried-angry eyes on Toria. He said, "You are never to come up here alone again, you understand? And you're sleeping in my room from now on."

"Maybe we *all* should," David said.

He thought about Xander, still asleep in their bedroom. A chair was wedged under the linen closet door handle, so that entrance into the house was probably secure, and most of the threats against them had come from the doors on the third floor, where they were now.

Xander's safe, he thought, but it still gave him the creeps thinking of his brother alone and asleep in this house. How much more defenseless can you be than when you were sleeping? That kicked his imagination into gear. He pictured towering figures standing around Xander's bed, hunched over him in the darkness.

He hopped off the bench. "Xander," he said. "We left him alone."

Dad stepped around Wuzzy to put an arm around David's shoulders. "He's fine. You're spooked."

"You bet I am," David said. Spooked, confused, frustrated, scared out of his pants for himself, his sister, his whole family: if it fell under the category of *This is a nightmare! Wake me up now!* David was feeling it. He said, "I thought . . . and Toria coming up here . . . I mean . . . what . . . why?"

"Exactly," Keal said. His rock-solid voice was like granite compared to the shifting sand of David's shaking words. "What and why? If whoever put the teddy bear up here wanted to lure Toria upstairs, what do they want and why do it this way? Why not just go downstairs, grab her, and run? That's more their style, right?"

"They surprised us before," Dad said. "When they took Gee—my wife—it happened so fast, we had no idea it was coming. Maybe they figured they couldn't do it like that again. As for why . . ." He shook his head. "I don't know. To drive us out of the house? Hold her until we leave?"

Toria's skin went a whiter shade of pale as he spoke. David slipped out from under Dad's arm and sat beside her. He nudged her with his shoulder and whispered, "It'll be all right."

She looked at him, unsure. She appeared tired and frightened and far from the bouncy, confident girl who was both funny and a pesky sister.

"Where did you last see it?" Keal said, nodding toward Wuzzy.

"The MCC," Dad said. "The night—" He frowned at David and Toria. "The night the big guy took Gee, Wuzzy recorded his voice."

"The big guy?" Keal said.

"Phemus," David said.

Keal nodded. "What did he say?"

"It was in some language I don't know," Dad said. "I've been meaning to find someone who can translate it, but . . . well, it's been pretty crazy around here."

Keal leaned over and snatched Wuzzy up by an ear.

"Careful," Dad said. "We don't want to erase what he said. Wuzzy could record new sounds over it."

"The switch is set to playback," Keal said, examining the panel on the bear's back. "How do you get it to speak?"

"Squeeze his paw," Toria said.

Mom's voice came out of the furry face, speaking Toria's name.

Despite having heard it minutes before, David felt like someone had given his heart a sharp poke. His breath turned into a lump and lodged in his throat. He swallowed hard and looked at Toria. She'd felt the poke, too: her eyes glistened. A drop ran down her cheek.

"Mom?" Xander yelled from down the hall. His footsteps reverberated through the floor. He hit the door frame. His hair was in a particularly messy state of bedhead. That and his wide eyes gave him the appearance of a wild man. He looked from face to face, disappointment deepening as he didn't find the one he had expected.

Dad stepped forward. "It's just a recording, son. Someone got hold of Wuzzy." He explained what had happened.

David knew his brother's pained expression matched his own.

"Could Mom . . ." Toria's voice trailed off. She was staring at Wuzzy again. "Could Wuzzy have recorded her *after* she was taken? Could that be her, you know, talking from wherever she is now?"

David's mouth dropped open. Mom—since she'd been taken? Someone would have had to take Wuzzy to her, then come back with it. Could finding her, reaching her, be that *easy*? Yesterday, when Xander had yelled at Phemus—*Where's our mother? Bring her back!*—David had thought it couldn't possibly be as simple as that. Because their own efforts to find her had been so difficult, dangerous, and futile, somewhere inside he'd assumed that's the way it was, that *no one* could just go get her. But Phemus could, couldn't he? Did he know where she was, even though it seemed that she was traveling from world to world? David wasn't sure how this could help, but it was *something*, a new possibility, a new reason to hope, a new—

"No," Xander said. "Wuzzy already had Mom's voice. That night, before she was taken. After Phemus scared Toria, David and I slept in her room with her. We all said good night. Mom, too. I checked the memory chip in Wuzzy and heard it. That was her saying good night to Toria."

David's shoulders slumped. *Of course*, he thought. As soon as the smallest spark started to rekindle his hope, something would stomp it out again. That's the way the house worked. That's the way their lives were these days.

He said, "It's mean, teasing us with Mom's voice. Like . . ." He searched for the word that described how he felt. "Like torture."

Keal nodded, thinking. "That may be it," he said. "Wartime tactic. A psychological assault. It's done all the time, in all kinds of ways: demoralize the enemy, crush their spirits so they don't have it in them to fight anymore. Maybe nobody was after Toria. Maybe they just wanted her or all of you to hear your mother's voice, get your hopes up, so they could be knocked down."

Somehow that was even worse, David thought. Intentionally hitting them in such a sensitive spot.

"Well," Xander said, his face tight, "it just ticks me off. It makes me want to fight harder."

"That's always the risk to using psychological warfare," Keal said. "It can backfire."

Dad let out a heavy breath and sat beside David. He patted the bench on his other side, and Xander sat too. They watched Keal. He was obviously thinking things through. The man had been a stranger to their family until last night, when he showed up with Jesse, but David felt he'd known him a lot longer. He'd heard that shared extreme experiences, especially involving life-and-death situations, drew people together quickly. They'd certainly had that: the fight with Phemus, the struggle getting out of the future world, saving Nana from getting sucked to the *Titanic*. David thought sharing their secrets about the house, the portals, and Mom's kidnapping also contributed to his feelings for Keal: the man had become an ally when they badly needed one.

Not a coincidence, he thought again.

Keal held Wuzzy by the ear and paced about the small room. Something about Toria's expression caught his eye, and he made a sweet face, totally out of sync with his stern, get-it-done appearance. He handed her the teddy bear, which she clutched close to her chest, and resumed pacing. Muscular as he was, and with the family seated in a line facing him, Keal seemed like a commander about to address his troops.

Except when he finally did, he sounded more like Mom: "You guys have school tomorrow, right?"

Dad nodded.

"But . . ." Xander started.

Keal stopped him. "Everybody back to bed."

David wished he had a camera for the expression on Xander's face.

CHAPTER

twenty-eight

THURSDAY, 5:05 A.M.

In his dream, David was in the third-floor hallway. He was opening door after door, looking in, moving to the next one. Every time he did, one of his family was standing in front of an open portal. Xander or Dad or Toria faced him, waved, then would get sucked backward through the portal, fast as a blink. It didn't bother him, though. He watched it happen, shut the door, went to the next one. Xander: no expression, just a wave, then he was gone. Dad: same thing. Then Toria. Over and over, door after door. Open, shut, open, shut. He started to feel the pull himself. He opened a door, saw Xander wave and then fly back through the portal. His shoulder pulled in toward the antechamber. He shut the door, but the tugging continued. Shaking him as he tried to walk.

He woke, felt the shake. Someone was leaning over him, shaking his shoulder. He jumped. "What—?"

"Shhhh."

The room was dark. Even the moonlight had stopped glowing through the window sheers.

"Xander?"

"It's me," a deep voice whispered. "Keal. Don't wake your brother."

"Keal?" David turned his head. He could barely make out Xander's form in bed, a blacker shadow against black shadows. The clock on the nightstand between their beds said it was still an hour before they had to get up. "What's going on?"

"You want to see Jesse?" Keal whispered.

"Now?"

"Best time. Hospitals are quiet this early. Just a few tired nurses. We'll sneak in, sneak out. Nobody the wiser. Your dad suggested I take you along."

"I feel like I was up all night, opening and shutting doors." David tossed his covers aside. "But yeah, sure. Let's do it."

"You and Jesse kind of hit it off, huh?"

"I like him," David said.

Xander moaned and rolled over.

David held his breath. He thought Keal did too.

As soon as Xander's breathing fell back into a slow rhythm, Keal whispered, "Get dressed. I'll meet you downstairs."

twenty-nine

THURSDAY, 5:33 A.M.

Keal and David squatted beside a metal door with the numeral 2 stenciled on it. They were on the landing at the top of a flight of concrete steps inside the hospital. It was the same place where David had his arm set in a plaster cast. This time, instead of rushing into the ER, David had waited outside the building while Keal found a way in. Keal had come back out a side door and led David up the stairs.

"He's probably sleeping," Keal whispered.

David frowned at him. "Sleeping . . . or unconscious, as in a coma?"

"That's one of the things I'm here to find out," Keal said. "I want to read his chart. You can see him for two minutes, that's all. Deal?"

David nodded. He wondered if Keal was sure Jesse had even made it through surgery, but he kept the question to himself.

Staying low, Keal turned the handle and eased the door open enough to peek through. He shut it again. "Okay, I'm going in. I'll find where he is, check for the staff, and come back for you. If I'm not back in five, get out of here. Oh . . ." He reached to a back pocket and produced a mobile phone. "It's your brother's. Call your dad. He'll come pick you up."

"What about you?" David said. He checked the phone and saw that someone had already turned off the ringer.

"Don't worry about me," Keal said. He winked, opened the door, and slipped through.

David backed into a corner. It was no place to hide, but he felt better with a wall on either side of him. It was crypt-quiet in the stairwell.

David pushed a button on the phone. The screen lit up, showing him the time. After an unblinking amount of time, waiting for a minute to click by, he lowered the phone. He knew it would be best if he didn't think about things: he'd only scare or worry himself into an upset stomach. But he could take only so much of listening to his own breathing, feeling his heart pound, staring at the mustard-colored walls of the stairwell. Soon his mind started churning.

What could happen that would prevent Keal from returning? If a nurse saw him, couldn't he just claim he was there to see a patient and didn't know when visiting hours were?

At five thirty in the morning? Probably not.

There was also a good chance the staff had been alerted to watch for him, the man who'd vanished after dropping off a stabbing victim. Jesse might have guards watching over him, just in case someone came to finish the job.

In Pinedale? David didn't think the town had enough cops to be so diligent. The hospital was small. He'd counted only a half dozen cars in the lot. The place might not even have its own security guard.

Maybe it was a trap! A sting!

Stop thinking, he told himself. *Keal knows what he's doing.*

I hope.

A noise rushed at him from the stairs. He slammed back, deeper into the corner. Water was flowing through pipes against an opposite wall; the pipes rattled in their brackets. Nothing more. After a few seconds, it stopped. Silence again.

How long had it been? A minute or two. No problem.

Under normal circumstances, sneaking in to see a relative after visiting hours wouldn't be such a big deal. They'd kick you out. But these weren't normal circumstances. Jesse was the victim of an attack. He'd been brought in by a stranger who hadn't stuck around. The town—because of Taksidian—was looking for reasons to get the Kings out of the house. Catching David here, now, could lead to all sorts of accusations, including charges that the family had hurt Jesse. Everything could come unraveled. They'd get arrested, taken away—Dad and Keal to jail, David and his brother and sister to juvenile detention or some child welfare facility. Mom would be gone. Forever.

Stop thinking!

David took a deep breath. He looked at the tops of his sneakers. Old Reeboks. Not his favorite Chucks. He'd lost one of them in the Civil War. That didn't even sound weird anymore. He wondered if he'd get it back. Didn't the worlds balance themselves out? What belonged there, went back; what belonged here, returned? Not the case with Mom. She—

The door clicked and opened.

Keal poked his head through. "Okay, come on," he whispered.

David went through the door and followed Keal down a long corridor. They tiptoed, but moved fast. Keal edged up to a corner, peered around it. He held his hand up. Then he slapped David's shoulder and darted forward. As David passed the other hallway, he saw a nurse walking away from him. He picked up his pace and nearly tripped over Keal.

Keal grabbed him and stepped close to a wall. "Just up

here. Through those double doors. It's the intensive care unit, so there's a nurses station front and center. There's a break room behind it. That's where the on-duty nurse was when I went in." He went to the doors, flashed his head past one of the windows set in them, then pushed through. David followed.

They ran straight for the nurses station, which looked like a fast-food counter. At a perpendicular hallway, Keal shot right. As they skirted past doors on either side, David heard noises behind him: an electronic chirping and then footsteps. Keal whipped through a door, David right on his heels.

David found himself standing at the foot of Jesse's bed. The old man looked like a deflated balloon: wrinkled and barely there. His skin matched the color of the stark white sheets. Blue veins made a road map of his cheeks, temples, and forehead. His closed eyes seemed too deeply recessed; David could make out the ridges of his skull around each socket.

Beside the bed, two IV bags hung from a chrome tree. A tube ran from each bag to his right arm. A machine mounted high on the wall beeped the rhythm of Jesse's heart. A mountain range, reflecting the recent history of his heartbeats, scrolled across a small screen. Various digital readouts flashed with changing numbers. Another contraption consisted of a transparent cylinder, inside which a bellows puffed up and sank down with each of Jesse's shallow breaths.

David wasn't sure if he should draw closer. Could he hurt

Jesse simply by being there? He imagined all sorts of infection-causing bacteria wafting from his lungs, off his skin, attacking Jesse's fragile body. There were so many machines, wires, and tubes—they seemed designed to ensnarl uninvited visitors. He turned his eyes to Keal, seeking permission.

"Go ahead," Keal whispered with a nod.

David went around to Jesse's left side, which looked free of medical clutter. Jesse's head lay on an uncomfortable-looking pillow. His arms were flat on the mattress, close to his sides.

This is what he'd look like in a coffin, David thought.

Stop!

He noticed now that tubes snaked into Jesse's nostrils. His lips were as white as his skin, making it seem he had no lips at all, only a tight line under his silver mustache. Cautiously, David reached for Jesse's hand. He stopped. It was bandaged—and incomplete. Where his index finger should have been, there was nothing. It was a gauze-wrapped gap, making the space between the thumb and fingers grotesquely wide. It looked like an alien hand. A faint red stain marked the spot.

David stared at his own index finger, imagined it gone, *taken*. A tear rolled down his cheek. "I'm sorry, Jesse," he whispered. He gently laid his hand over the old man's.

Jesse pulled in a jagged breath.

David gasped. He swung his head to Keal, who was standing at the foot of the bed. Keal looked up from the clipboard in his hand and smiled.

When David retuned his gaze to Jesse, the old man's eyelids were fluttering. They closed, then opened halfway. His irises were the bluest David had ever seen, even more than Dad's and Xander's, which he'd always thought were movie-star perfect. Those sapphires angled toward David, and Jesse's mustache trembled.

"Jesse," David said. He blinked, and the tears fell.

Jesse's lips parted, then closed again. His eyes did the opposite: they closed, then opened.

"Don't try to talk," David whispered. "It's okay."

The old man moved his head slightly one direction, then the other: no.

No? No what? It's not okay?

Jesse said, "Dae." The word was so airy and weak, it reminded David of a wisp of smoke.

"I'm so sorry, Jesse," David said. A fat teardrop splattered on the old man's thin arm. "You came to help us, and . . . and . . ." He sniffed.

Another almost nonexistent word eased out of Jesse's mouth: "Stay."

David snapped his head around to Keal. "He wants us to stay."

"Can't, David," Keal said quietly.

"But . . ." When he looked, Jesse's eyes were closed, and his head was moving again: again, *no.*

"No?" David said. "Don't stay?"

167

Jesse caught David in his eyes. They were so vivid, so alive, so unlike the body in which they were housed. His eyebrows slowly came together. David realized Jesse was giving him all the strength he had.

The old man said, "Stay . . . together." He blinked slowly. "You . . . and . . . Xan . . ." He inhaled, exhaled, inhaled. "Xander. Stay . . . together."

"Xander and me?" David said. "We should stay together?"

Jesse's head moved again, this time barely up and barely down.

"When? *All the time?*"

Jesse said, "Come . . . see . . . me."

"I'm here," David said. "I came. You want Xander too?"

Jesse's eyes were closed, his lips parted.

"Jesse?"

David would have thought Jesse had died, if it weren't for the bellows in the clear cylinder. It slowly expanded, contracted, expanded. David looked at Keal, who nodded.

"Come . . ." Jesse wheezed. His eyes remained close. "See . . . me."

"We will, Jesse. We'll come together."

"I think," Keal whispered, "the two things are separate. He said 'stay.' Stay with your brother. And then, another thing: come see him."

"But I'm here," David said. "Does he mean come again? Keep coming?"

Keal shrugged.

"Can we? Can we come back?"

"If we don't get caught." Keal hung the clipboard on a hook attached to the foot of the bed. "We have to go."

David returned his attention to Jesse. The man was still. It was almost as though he'd never been awake at all, never spoken or looked at David.

"Jesse?" David bent his fingers around his hand, down low, by the thumb. He gave it a little squeeze. "I'll stay with Xander," he said, though he wasn't sure what that meant. "And I'll come back. I'll come see you. I will."

CHAPTER

thirty

THURSDAY, 6:22 A.M.

"Where's Dae?" Xander said, walking into the kitchen.

Dad looked up from the stove, where he was flipping French toast. The smell made Xander realize how hungry he was. Dad said, "He and Keal went to see Jesse."

"Now? Why?" Xander opened the refrigerator and grabbed a carton of orange juice.

"Keal thought this early they could get in and out without

being seen." Dad held up a spatula with a fat, golden slice. "Want some?"

"Sure." He poured three glasses. Toria should be down soon. He said, "I want to see Jesse."

Dad said, "You just don't want to go to school."

"You got that right," Xander said. "You know, if I stayed home, I could help Keal get the walls back up and—"

"Don't start." Dad pushed a paper plate with a stack of toast across the island counter. He used the spatula to point at a bottle of syrup. "You know we can't risk people snooping into why any of us aren't doing what's expected. School, job, anything."

Xander snatched up the plate and headed toward the foyer. He said, "Is David going to miss?"

"They should be back any minute," Dad said. "Where are you going?"

"To get ready for school," Xander said. On the way up the stairs, Xander balanced the plate on the glass, folded a piece of toast, and bit it in half. He stopped at the top. He could hear the shower through the bathroom door. So much for brushing his teeth, fixing his hair, scrubbing his face.

He thought about waiting in the chair that was wedged under the linen closet door handle, the one Keal had used to play sleep police. He had to admit that Keal had been right: Xander felt much better than he had last night. Once he finally got to sleep, it was deep and dreamless. He was still anxious about getting to all the things they had to do, but he felt less panicked about doing them all at once.

One step at a time, he thought. *As long as we keep stepping. No stopping. Keep moving. Hang in there, Mom, we're coming. We are.*

He couldn't believe they had to go to school. He understood the logic of keeping up appearances, especially if it took a long time to find Mom—and it was starting to feel like it would take awhile. But it's not the way he would have handled it. If he were Dad, he'd quit his job. He'd sell the 4Runner and everything else they had to get enough cash for food and whatever they needed to make the house secure—to *fortify* it, as Dad had said. He'd register the kids for home-schooling. Then he'd spend every waking minute finding Mom. Was anything else more important?

If he were Dad, he'd do a lot of things differently. Then again, if he were Dad, they wouldn't be in this mess.

This sucks, he thought. Just like being forced to go to bed last night sucked. Maybe he should get a T-shirt with those two words on it. David had told him he felt like the family slogan was *Nothing we can do.* But that wasn't true. There were a lot of things they could do, if only they were allowed to do them. Not being able to do them—because of sleep or school or because this or that was too dangerous—fell firmly under *his* slogan: *This sucks.*

Forget waiting, he thought, turning away from the chair. He carried his breakfast past Mom and Dad's bedroom and stopped at the junction of the two hallways on the second floor. The walls at the end of the short hall lay on the floor. Plaster dust, wood, wiring were scattered all over them. Fixing them would take more than simply pushing them back into place. They would need new wiring, studs, wallboard. A lot of work. See? So much to do.

He squatted to set his plate and glass on the floor. He pushed the second half of the French toast into his mouth, then took a drink. Behind him, the shower turned off. He could hear Dad banging around in the kitchen.

Xander made up his mind.

He rose and looked over his shoulder at the empty main hallway. Then he walked over the fallen walls as quietly as possible. At the base of the stairs leading to the hallway of doors, he didn't pause. He went up two steps at a time.

CHAPTER

thirty-one

THURSDAY, 6:50 A.M.

On the ride home from the hospital, David thought about
Jesse and how what Taksidian had done to him could have
happened to any of them. So when he walked through the
front door to see his father coming out of the kitchen, he ran
to him and squeezed him tightly. He pushed his face into
Dad's chest, feeling the solidness of it, so unlike Jesse's
almost-not-there condition. He turned his head, pressed his

ear to Dad's shirt, and listened to his heart. Dad hugged him back, holding him like he was never going to let go.

"Dae," Dad said. "Are you all right? Is Jesse—?"

"He's alive," Keal said behind David. "He spoke to David."

"He did? He's that well?"

"Not really," Keal said. "He didn't say much, and it took a lot out of him. I'm not sure he had that much to give. I read his chart."

"And . . . ?" Dad said.

Keal didn't answer. David suspected he shook his head to indicate *not good.*

Dad's arms tightened. "I'm sorry, Dae. But he spoke. That's a good sign. What'd he say?"

David released his hold and took a step back. "He said Xander and I should stay together."

Dad looked puzzled. "What does that mean?"

"I don't know," David said. "Maybe he knows something . . . about the future." He shook his head. "Maybe he thinks something's going to try to separate us."

"Or he knows you need each other," Keal said. "Stay together, like the buddy system."

"Yeah," Dad said. "We talked about that, remember?"

"And he said to come see him," David said.

"In the hospital?" Dad said. "He wants us to visit?"

David shrugged. "I guess. He wasn't making a lot of sense."

"What else did he say?"

"That's it." David looked around his father to the kitchen. "Where's Xander?"

"In the bathroom, I think."

"No, he's not," Toria said, coming down the stairs. She rounded the newel. "I was just in there."

"Xander!" David called.

Dad gripped his shoulder. "You hungry?"

"Not really," David said, starting for the stairs.

"I am!" Toria said.

As David passed her, he gave her a short hug.

"What was that for?" she said.

He climbed up the stairs, smiling over the railing. "Just because."

At the top, he turned toward Xander's and his bedroom. He pulled Xander's mobile phone out of his back pocket wanting to give it to him before he forgot. He called his brother's name.

His brain caught up with something he had glimpsed, and he stopped. In the other direction, on the floor at the end of the hallway: a glass and a paper plate.

"Xander?" He walked to the items and squatted. The glass was half-full of OJ and the plate held a piece of French toast. He set the phone on the floor beside them and stepped into the MCC. Empty. "Hey, Xander!"

Back in the hall, he eyed the fallen walls. Footprints were in the dust, but they could have been from last night, when all of them had gone upstairs. Still . . . that catchphrase of Han Solo's came to mind: *I got a bad feeling about this.* Xander had used it when they'd first found the house.

Should've trusted the feeling then, David thought. *Should trust it now.*

"Dad!" he called. He could hear Dad, Keal, and Toria talking in the kitchen. "Dad!" He walked over the walls and stopped at the bottom of the stairs. "Xander, you up there?"

Just a look, he told himself, going up. The lights were on in the crooked, third-floor hallway. "Xander, are you—"

"Here!" Xander's voice came at him from one of the antechambers.

"Xander? Where are you?"

Xander stepped out of a room at the far end of the hall. "Come here," he said. "Quick." He disappeared again.

"Wait!" David said. "What are you doing?" He looked down the stairs. He could no longer hear the conversation from the kitchen. "Dad!" he called as loudly as his lungs could push the word out.

"David!" Xander was back in the hall. "Will you just come here for a second? Look at this?"

Reluctantly, David started for him. Xander ducked into the room.

When David reached the open antechamber, Xander was putting on a hat. No, not a hat, David realized. A *helmet.*

"What are you *doing?*" David said.

"This is it," Xander said. "The place Jesse was trying to tell us about."

David looked at the items still hanging from the hooks, a pair of tattered leather lace-up slippers on the bench. "How do you figure?"

Xander pointed to the helmet. It was a battered thing that looked like it had been pieced together from scraps of metal. "What does this look like?"

"A helmet," David said. "The last time you put one on, you went to the Roman Colosseum. You almost got yourself killed."

"David!" Xander said, exasperated. He snatched off the helmet and held it upside down. At the front, the two metal pieces were bent up, as though they had caught a fierce blow and didn't quite break off. Xander used his finger to trace the arc of the helmet, then the two squarish metal plates. "Jesse's drawing," he said. "The thing you said looked like buck teeth."

David squinted at it. "I don't know," he said slowly.

"And look." Xander pointed to the corner of the room, where a weapon rested on the bench, its handle propped up into the corner. "An ax! I told you the symbol was an ax. And *this* . . ." He resettled the helmet over his head and pulled a leather pouch off a hook. He shook a couple medallions out into his palm. He turned one over and held it up to David. "What does that look like?"

"A house," David said. It was engraved into the medallion.

"All three of the symbols Jesse left for us," Xander said. "This has to be it."

David wasn't so sure. He said, "But the helmet . . . Xander, why didn't he draw a helmet and not just a curve with two squares?"

"He was injured," Xander said. "He drew only what would help us distinguish this helmet from any other. I've never seen anything like it before, have you?"

David shook his head. "So, what? You're just going over?"

"If we leave now, the world might be gone when we get back. It was important enough for Jesse to use his own . . ." He frowned. "To use his own blood to get the message to us."

"Wait here," David said. "I'll go get Dad."

"He'll say, 'Let's do it after school,'" Xander said. He tied the pouch to his belt. Then he leaned past David and picked up the ax. "It could be now or never. I say now."

"This isn't right, and you know it!" David leaned into the hallway. "Dad! Dad! Toria! Keal!"

A chilly wind blew over him, carrying bits of hay or grass. Xander had opened the door. He was standing in front of the portal, one hand on the edge of the door, the other holding the ax. His hair coming out from under the helmet fluttered in the breeze. On the other side, the wind must have been more severe; David could hear it howling.

"Xander, wait!" David yelled. "You don't know what's over there!"

Xander looked over his shoulder. "Jesse's not going to send us someplace dangerous, Dae."

He would have if he thought it would help us find Mom, David thought. But that would make Xander even more determined. Instead he said, "An ax and a helmet? Come on!"

He wanted to reach for Xander, grab his waistband, and tug him back away from the portal. But his brother was bigger and stronger. He could easily shake David loose. Or worse: pull him through with him. The thought struck him hard.

He said, "I talked to Jesse. He said we should stay together. Xander, maybe this is what he meant."

Xander smiled. "Then come on."

"No, not like this," David pleaded. "Let's get Dad, then I'll go with you. Please."

"Now or never, Dae."

"Dad!" David yelled again into the hallway.

"Go get him," Xander said.

David felt relief washed over him. And with Xander's next words, it was gone, chased away by sickening fear.

Xander said, "I'll meet you over there. Come when you're ready."

"No! Wait!" David was certain this was what Jesse had meant: not that this was the place he wanted them to go, but that they had to stay together—now. "I'll go," he said.

He turned to the items left on the hooks and the bench. He could have followed Xander through without selecting his own, but if they did get separated, he'd have nothing to guide him to the portal home. He grabbed a silver bracelet and slipped it onto his wrist. It was way too big. He moved it to the other arm and pushed it snugly over the bandage Dad had wrapped around his cast. He pulled down a spool of yarn wrapped around a wooden dowel. He sat on the bench, kicked off his sneakers, and tugged on the slipperlike shoes.

Cinching the laces tight, he glanced at Xander. "Do you smell smoke?"

Xander sniffed. "No." Then he did something that shook David to his bones. He waved and fell backward through the portal.

Just as he had in David's dream.

CHAPTER

thirty-two

David belly flopped onto hard-packed earth. His cheek smacked down, and so did his broken arm—of course. Didn't going through the portals *always* result in jarring the part of his body that hurt the most? The pain flared up into his shoulder like fire.

He groaned and rolled onto his back, hugging his cast. He spat dirt out of his mouth. It was in his eyes too. He rubbed them and blinked. Above him was a ceiling made of branches, twigs, and straw. Thatch, he thought it was called. Glancing around, he saw that he was in a cottage of sorts: plank walls; a stone fireplace that appeared to have been cobbled together by a child; table, chairs, and bed frame, all made from rough-hewn logs. Tools, clothes, wooden goblets were among the litter scattered around him.

He rubbed his shoulder, then his arm. Holding his cast above him, he gave the bracelet a good look. It was designed to resemble a coiled snake. Its head was wide and flat, its eyes wicked. Two fangs jutted out of an open mouth.

Great, he thought. Not exactly a peaceful symbol. What had his brother gotten them into?

Beside him, Xander was pushing himself into a sitting position. He moaned and said, "Rough landing."

David rolled onto his side and punched Xander in the ribs, hard.

"Oww!" Xander yelped. "What was that for?"

Not ten minutes ago, Toria had asked David that same thing, but it was because he had given her a hug. "For being stupid," David said. "For breaking your promise to Dad that you wouldn't sneak into the other worlds anymore. For making me come with you. For—"

"Hey, I didn't make you do anything."

"Right, Xander," David said. He hoisted himself off the ground. "I'm going to just let you go alone. After Jesse said we should say together. You could have waited five minutes for Dad."

"Five minutes?" Xander said. He stooped to pick up the ax. He touched his head, and David saw the helmet had come off. Xander looked around for it. "More like eight hours. Then it could have been gone."

David punched him again.

"Stop hitting me!" Xander shoved him.

David tripped and went down on his butt. "That was for going over like you did," he said. "Waving and falling backward. What was that?"

Xander smiled and shrugged. "That's the way scuba divers go into the ocean, backward off the boat. I figured, why not? We usually wipe out when we come over anyway. What's the big deal?"

David shook his head. "Never mind." He turned to look out through an open door at rolling meadows and a woods in the distance. The nippy breeze he had felt coming through the portal was now coming through the cottage door. "Where are we?"

"Don't know," Xander said. "Hey." He pointed at his helmet on the ground. It was rolling toward the doorway. "And isn't that yours?"

The spool of yarn. David hadn't realized he'd dropped it. It was heading for the door as well.

"Are they heading for the portal home?" David said. "So soon?"

Xander darted forward and snatched up the two items, which had almost met each other on their way out. He handed the spool to David.

David watched as a length of yarn lifted and fluttered against the breeze. It pointed at the door. He said, "I thought the longer we're here, the stronger the pull. I haven't felt it so soon before."

"Maybe we're not supposed to be here," Xander said.

"What? You say that *now*?" If he weren't sitting on the ground, David thought he might have punched him again. "You said, 'This is the place! This is it!'"

"It still may be where Jesse wants us to be," Xander said. "But maybe Time doesn't."

David sighed and said, "We don't know enough to be doing this."

"This is how we learn." Xander extended a hand to him.

David glared at him.

Xander said, "I'm sorry, okay? I just want to rescue Mom so badly, and I'm afraid we're running out of time. It drives me crazy, all the waiting and preparing, sleeping and keeping up appearances. I just want to go for it, you know?"

"You're right about one thing," David said, grabbing his brother's hand. "You are crazy."

Xander leaned down to push on the bed's mattress. It was straw with a loose covering of stitched-together animal hides. He said, "You won't say that if we find what Jesse wants us to find. Maybe it's the key to everything, something that will help us rescue Mom, save the world, and get out of that house once and for all."

"I doubt it," said David. "If there was something like that, he would have told us before. I think it'll help us, but not solve all our problems."

Xander said, "You never can—"

"Shhhh," David said. "Hear that?"

He realized that what he'd thought was the sound of wind from the other side of the portal was actually voices. A chorus of screaming voices. Over them, like the cracking of a whip, were sharp, high-pitched shrieks. They rose, then broke into stuttering laughter.

David's skin went cold. He turned big eyes to Xander. "What *is* that?"

Xander shook his head.

"And I *definitely* smell smoke," David told him. He could see it now as well. Gray swirls came through the door and began to gather into a cloud, away from the gustiness outside. He moved closer to Xander and grabbed his arm. "I don't think Jesse would send us to a place where people scream like they're being torn apart and something's on fire."

Xander moved toward the door. David clung to his arm, shuffling behind him. They stepped out of the cottage. The screaming pierced David's ears; the smoke stung his nostrils. He swept his gaze over the hills and woods. Then he saw a towering stone building, a castle. It was a couple of hundred yards away. Beyond it, an ocean.

The two boys edged to the corner. More thatch-roofed cottages dotted the landscape in a sweeping arc behind the one into which the portal had deposited him and Xander. The cottages were arranged in a crescent around the castle, on one side of it and behind it. Theirs was the last one in line.

Thank goodness for that much of a break, David thought—for all but the closest cottages were blazing, their straw roofs feeding huge fires, like flaming hair on wood faces. People were yelling and running: some into the hills and woods farther from the castle, some toward the fortress. But by far, a greater number of people had already fallen: their bodies pocked the field between the cottages and castle as though a giant hand had scattered them like seeds.

A roar of voices rose up some distance away.

"It's some kind of siege on the castle," Xander said. "Probably from the sea. The front of the castle's on the other side. These are just the peasants' huts."

"If the assault is on the other side," David said, "what happened here? What killed those people?"

As he spoke, a man broke from one of the cottages. He ran toward the castle as though demon dogs were on his scent. In the next instant, David saw the thing that was after the man, and it turned out to be much worse than mere demon dogs.

A beast sprang from between two cottages. It was tall, with

the head of a wolf and the body of a bear. It loped on its hind legs. It carried a sword as thick and long as an arm. The thing bellowed, howled, and barked as it went after the running man.

David screamed. It felt as though his organs compressed within his body, pulling in for safety.

Xander clamped his hand over David's mouth. "Shhhh," he said. "He hasn't spotted us." He dropped down and yanked on David's shirt.

David collapsed to the ground, flat on his belly. He couldn't take his eyes off the beast. The thing's gait was wild and ungainly, but fast. It was gaining on the man.

"Run," David whispered. The man had halved the distance to the castle. David couldn't see an entrance, but there must have been one that the man knew about. Either that, or the guy was blind with fear and simply running—not *to* anything, but *away* from the beast. David understood. *Run, run!*

The man tripped. He crashed and slid, kicking up dust and grass. He looked back, screamed, scrambled to get up. "Come on, come on," David whispered.

"Shh!" Xander said sharply.

The man was up, his legs moving, moving. But the beast was on him. It didn't swing the sword, as David had expected, but lunged through the air, landing on the man's back. They went down together. The beast's sword hand rose and came down, hilt first. He pounded and pounded. Then his massive

Robert Liparulo

wolf head lowered to the man's throat. The head shook like a dog ripping at a bone.

David dropped his face into the dirt. His breathing came fast. He knew he was hyperventilating, but he couldn't stop himself. He breathed in dirt, coughed it out.

Xander pulled David's head into his armpit. "David! Shhhh!"

"What—" David spat the word out with muddy globules. He forced himself to lower his voice. "What is that thing? That beast?"

"A berserker," Xander whispered. "An elite Viking warrior. He's wearing a wolf's head like a hat. His cloak is bearskin. He's just a man."

"A man?" David said, pulling his head from Xander's grasp. "He's *eating* that guy."

"Crawl back," Xander said. "Stay low."

They began sliding backward on the ground. The beast—the berserker—was standing over his victim now, hacking at him with the sword.

Xander whispered, "They were known for their ruthlessness in battle. They were insane. Sometimes the Norse ships that carried them would put ashore at a village they had no intention of attacking, just so the berserkers could vent their rage on the villagers. So they wouldn't turn on each other."

David groaned. "You said berserkers. More than one?"

"Oh, yeah," Xander said. "They were organized in what we would call platoons."

Platoons of those things? David thought. *Platoons?*

"Stop!" Xander said. "Down!" He squeezed his eyes shut and pushed his cheek into the ground.

"What?" David said. Then he saw: the berserker was standing, his shoulders rising and falling, panting from the exertion of having just killed a man.

And he was staring straight at them.

CHAPTER

thirty-three

"He sees us!" David said.

Xander raised his head.

The berserker lifted his faces—the wolf face and the human one, which was so drenched in red, David could see it glistening from a hundred yards away. He let loose a howl, which became a scream, which turned into a hyenalike laugh. He loped toward the boys.

"Run!" Xander said. He got to his feet and pulled David up.

As he rose, David watched the berserker drawing toward them. That wolf head bobbed up and down like a prancing pony's. The sword made huge circles in the air beside the man, as though it were a propeller enabling him to fly across the field. To David, he *was* flying, closing the distance faster than any man should.

Movement caught his eye, and David forced himself to look away from the berserker. More of the insane warriors, all of them with animal heads—some wolf, some bear— loped out from among the burning cottages into the field behind the first berserker. One was dragging a body by the foot. Together, as though through a shared consciousness, they turned toward David and Xander and started running.

The brothers scrambled back. David broke away from Xander and shot into the cottage.

"David, no!" Xander said. He grabbed hold of the door frame. "Not here," he said. "They'll break in, burn us out."

The berserker screamed—so close, David braced himself against the back wall for the inevitable: that thing crashing into Xander.

Xander held out his hand. "Come on, Dae!" he said. "Maybe we can make it to the castle!"

David couldn't move. He shook his head.

His brother's eyes flashed wide. He stepped inside and slammed the door. He pushed his back to it. David squinted, waiting for the impact on the other side. Three seconds . . . five . . . ten.

"Xander . . ." David whispered.

His brother stepped away from the door.

A sword broke through where Xander's head had been. Instead of pulling it out to strike again, the berserker moved the sword in a sharp, jerking motion. The wood under it split and broke. David couldn't imagine the strength it took to cut through a solid wood door with a straight-edged broadsword.

David stuttered his brother's name. He shot a look around the interior: no place to escape, no place to hide.

Xander flashed crazy eyes at him. He said, "We have to make a stand."

"What? No!"

Xander's desperate expression said, *What choice do we have?* He drew close and put his back to David. He clutched the ax in both fists and raised it above his head.

"Xander," David said.

"Yeah?"

"I think I peed my pants," David said. "No, I'm okay."

Xander scowled over his shoulder. "You're cracking jokes? *Now?*"

"I wasn't joking."

The sword kept cutting—*ripping* through the door.

They could hear the howls and screaming of the other berserkers. Getting loud. Getting close.

"They're coming," Xander said.

David tried to squirm out from between his brother and the wall. He had no idea what he was going to do, but he had to do *something*. He had to *move*.

Xander pushed back harder. He swung his arm around to keep David in place. "No, David. Wait . . . wait . . ."

The screeching voices continued.

"Maybe they'll attack the other cottages first," David said. *As if one at the door isn't enough to turn us into hamburger.*

"We can hope they turn on each other," Xander said. "Like I read they sometimes did, waiting to fight."

"Not when they have us to fight," David said. But he really didn't think the slaughter of kids would amount to much of a fight.

Xander glanced back at David. "Sorry, Dae. I should have listened to you."

"We would have wound up here sooner or later," David said.

When the sword was knee-high, the berserker withdrew it. The gash in the door was jagged, an inch wide and four feet long. The wolf face *thunk*ed against the wood. Its nose was pressed to the gash, as though sniffing for fear.

Plenty of it in here, David thought.

Below the snout, a man's eye peered at them. The iris was a thin blue halo around a huge pupil. All around it, the eye was bloodshot—more red than white.

"Go away!" Xander screamed. He made like he was swinging the ax.

The eye, the snout, whipped out of sight.

"They say werewolf legends came from berserkers," Xander said.

David nudged him. "How do you know so much?"

Xander smiled back at him. "I wrote a paper on them last year." He took a step toward the door.

"Xander!"

"Just looking." Keeping the ax high, he stepped right to the gash in the door. He put his face to it. "I don't see—"

There was an explosion of human-kinetic energy on the side wall: wall one second, man the next. The berserker had hit it with so much force, planks splintered and whole boards spun into the room. The thing paused just long enough to lock eyes on David.

In that moment, David took him in: the wolf head had torn off and was flopping against his back; his hairy face dripped blood, which stained his muscular chest; his shirt had been torn into strips that now dangled over his belt to his knees; the bearskin cloak hung off his shoulders like wings. His beard parted, revealing a gaping maw of yellow, canted teeth. He screamed.

So did David. It was loud and high-pitched, and he continued pushing it out as he scrambled backward along the wall.

The berserker leaped and came down directly in front of him.

The stench of wet animals, body odor, and raw meat assaulted David's senses.

The berserker seized David's neck with powerful fingers. He leaned in, and all David saw was mouth and teeth.

CHAPTER

thirty-four

David turned his face away. He clamped his eyes closed.

The berserker fell into him, and instinctively, David side-stepped. The beast knocked against David's shoulder and kept falling. It hit the wall and collapsed to the floor.

His brother had clobbered the beast. Xander was standing behind where the berserker had been, hefting the ax for another blow. His eyes were almost as wild as the berserker's.

David raised his hands. "You got him! You got him!"

Xander lowered the ax. His shoulders went up and down with heavy breaths.

David looked down at the collapsed man. "I think you killed him."

"No," Xander said. "I hit him with the flat of the blade, like a club. I didn't have time to position it right."

"Well, it worked," David said.

"A blow like that couldn't have killed him. Not this guy."

A scream reached them. Through the broken wall, they saw a berserker storm out of a nearby cottage, swinging a sword over his head and plunging the blade down into the earth. His face snapped toward the boys. He howled in rage, tore the weapon out of the ground, and started for them.

"Come on." Xander ran for the door. He hit it with his shoulder. The section between the gash and the edge broke away, and he was outside.

As David crossed the small room, the man who had attacked him began making noises. He was facedown on the floor, a shoulder and arm banked up against the back wall. He shook his head furiously, growling. His legs began to move, sliding over the hard dirt floor. David darted through the door.

"Feel the pull?" Xander asked.

David's feet wanted to slide out from under him, as though he were standing on ice. The leather slippers were pulling toward the portal home. The snake bracelet as well tugged at his arm as firmly as a human hand. He realized he was still gripping the spool of yarn—somehow.

"Yeah," David said. "That way, toward the far corner of the castle. But that other berserker's coming to, and they're crazy-fast, man."

"Give me that," Xander said, grabbing for the spool. He took it from David and tossed it. In midair it changed direction and spun toward the castle. It hit the ground, bounced, and tumbled away. Xander pointed. "Go for it, soccer boy."

David ran. The spool was faster than any soccer ball he'd ever chased. He lowered his head and pushed harder. He heard Xander closer behind.

"Is he . . . is he gaining?"

"Don't look, Dae, just run. We can't get back if we lose that yarn. Go!"

"What?" David said. "I thought . . . we just had to . . . follow it . . . to the portal."

"Shut up and run."

David poured everything into his legs. The ground passed under him faster than he could remember it ever doing. He wondered if the slippers were helping, or if it was just easier to run *after* something instead of *from* something. He remembered thinking that the berserker's first victim may not have been running toward a shelter as much as he was simply trying to get away. That strategy hadn't worked. The man had been caught . . . and eaten.

David's feet faltered. He was about to tumble, he could feel it.

No . . . no . . . run!

He pinwheeled his right arm and his broken left as much as it allowed him to do. He forced his upper body back slightly. His feet caught up, and he was running, not falling, running.

Don't think about what you saw, he thought. *Don't think about anything but catching that spool.*

It tumbled and spun ten feet ahead of him. The ground began its ascent toward the castle. David pushed harder.

Leave it all on the field, his coach used to tell him. *If you've got energy after the game, you didn't try hard enough.*

His legs were aching now. His lungs screamed for more air than he could give them. He felt a stitch just sparking to life in his side.

"Xan . . ." he said. "Xander?"

"Go, go," his brother said. Farther behind than he had been, but not by much.

Something sailed passed him. It *thunk*ed into the ground and wobbled. David ran past it.

"A spear? A *spear?*" he yelled.

"He . . . only had . . . one. Go!"

But he's close enough to throw it past us!

Here David had thought he was giving Dash from *The Incredibles* a run for his money, and that thing was keeping up! Gaining!

The spool tumbled up to the corner of the castle and around it. David was right on it. He rounded the corner and stopped.

Xander's footsteps pounded behind him. He hit the corner and crashed into David.

David flew forward, fell.

His brother was already over him, picking him up. He didn't have to ask why David had stopped; they both could see: Vikings, hundreds of them. They swarmed the castle walls, pouring up from the endless blue ocean a half mile from the front of the castle. Their ships—narrow and long, with dragonhead prows—were grounded on the shore. The warriors had come around to this side of the castle and were heading toward the rear—directly at David and Xander.

The spool flipped over the ground, bouncing its way to the Vikings.

Then the warriors' front line blurred. The Vikings closest to them went out of focus and wavered. The spool popped up and vanished.

"Come on," David said. He ran straight for the fighting men.

"Wait," Xander said.

He screamed, and David looked back.

That hadn't been Xander's scream, not then: it came from the berserker standing behind him. Its wolf head looked over Xander. The beast howled and swung its sword.

Then Xander screamed—and ducked. The blade cut the air over his head. It clanged and sparked against the stone castle wall.

The berserker kicked, sending Xander tumbling.

David grabbed him and helped him up. They ran, just ahead of the beast.

"I see it," Xander said.

Beyond the glimmering, rippling portal, a Viking faced them. He hefted a spear and threw it.

David leaped into its path.

CHAPTER

thirty-five

THURSDAY, 7:25 A.M.

Another belly flop. This time David came down on the hardwood floor of the antechamber. Banged chin, jolted broken
arm, wind forced out of his lungs. But he remembered to roll
away so Xander wouldn't land on him. He turned and
watched a spear sail out of the portal. It *thunk*ed into the
antechamber's hallway door, where it vibrated with energy.

Keal, sitting on the bench, stared up at it with huge eyes.

Xander toppled out of the portal. He landed on his shoulder, somersaulted, and sprang up, rapping his head on the spear.

"The door!" he yelled. "Shut the door!"

David spun on the floor, grabbed the edge of the portal door, and pulled. He slid toward it, but it didn't budge. Xander straddled him, putting his own strength into the effort. Keal joined them.

"It . . . won't . . ." Xander said, groaning.

Then the door did shut. It swung around faster than any of them could have slammed it.

Keal jumped back.

Something came through the portal, and the door pinned it against the frame.

"What the—" Keal said.

Jutting between door and jamb was the heavy blade of a double-edged sword. It quivered under the pressure of the door. Then it snapped and clattered onto the floor. The door slammed.

Panting for breath, David gaped at the blade. He looked up at Xander. "You okay?"

"Little sore." He lifted his shirt. His ribs were bruised in the perfect shape of a foot. "Could be worse, I guess." He swiveled his head. The spear sticking out of the hallway door was even with his eyes.

Keal stood on the other side of the shaft. He scanned the

weapon from spearhead out. He scowled at Xander, then down at David. "You boys are in *big* trouble."

Xander turned away from him to frown at David. He held out his hand and pulled him up. David immediately bent over to put his hands on his knees. His stomach churned, but he didn't know if it was because of the carnage he'd witnessed or the physical exertion or all the adrenaline, fear, and relief coursing through his blood. He felt Xander's hand on his back.

"How long were we gone?" Xander said.

"Long enough to really tick off your dad," Keal said. "He couldn't believe you went over. He left to attend an important faculty meeting. Besides, there was nothing he could do. The two of you took all the items, so he couldn't open the door."

"I'm glad he couldn't come over," David said, staring at the floor between the leather slippers.

Oh, just barf, he told himself. *You'll feel better, and these guys won't care.*

Xander leaned down close. He whispered, "It's okay, Dae. Sit down." He guided David to the bench.

David sat. "I'm all right," he said, not sure it was true.

"What happened over there?" Keal said.

"Can I cuss?" Xander said.

"No."

"Then I have nothing to say."

Keal looked like he was going to smack him. He glanced

at David and saw the smile David couldn't keep his lips from forming. Keal grinned—against his wishes, it seemed to David. Their humor spread to Xander, who actually laughed.

A wind blew in from under the door.

"Here it comes," David said.

"This ought to be interesting," Xander said, eyeing the spear.

The wind swirled around the room. It plucked the grass and dirt off of David and Xander. Their hair and clothes billowed as it searched and collected. David even felt it brushing through his eyelashes, looking for particles that belonged to that ancient, violent time on the other side of the portal. He wondered what would happen if they ate in the other worlds. He felt queasy again, but he was too curious to let it distract him.

The sword blade rattled against the floor, then disappeared under the door.

"What about those?" Keal said, pointing at an ax and helmet on the floor. Xander had dropped them when he came through.

"They belong here," Xander said. He picked up the helmet and placed it on a hook.

The spear began to shake. It wobbled like a Richter needle before popping out of the hallway door. It hit the portal door, flipped in the air, and slammed down as if thrown.

"Xander," Keal said, "back against the wall."

The wooden shaft hit the bottom of the portal door. It began splintering, disintegrating. Slowly, the spearhead drew closer to the crack: five feet . . . four . . . three.

The three of them were looking at the tip, not the shaft, as it scraped across the floor. It was flat, with a wide, circular flange that gripped the shaft. It also boasted small wings, like fins, that must have stabilized it in flight. The flange and the wings, which were perpendicular to the flat blade, were way too wide to fit under the door.

"What's it made out of?" David said.

"Iron," said Xander. "Usually folded and hammered to make it especially strong. The Vikings knew how to make weapons."

"Let's get outta here," Keal said.

Xander said, "You think it's going to explode?"

"Who knows?"

Xander gave him a knowing smile. "You don't want to leave."

The flange thumped against the door. The spearhead trembled. Then the flange began to melt. David thought he could see a razor-thin line of orange metal where the spearhead touched at the door. More obvious was the liquidation of the iron. He imagined that pushing a candle into a blowtorch would look like this. The flange slid into the door, dissolving as it did. Then it was gone.

The three of them stared at the spot where the last of it had disappeared under the door.

"Well," Xander said, "I'm glad the door *opens* when Time wants a person."

thirty-six

THURSDAY, 7:34 A.M.

"I gotta take you to school," Keal said. They were still in the antechamber: David on the bench, Xander and Keal standing.

"Come on!" Xander said. "Do you know what we just went through?"

"You knew you had school, Xander. I promised your dad."

"David's going to puke," Xander said.

"Xander—" David said. He didn't want to be a tool in Xander's manipulation.

But Keal had it covered. "Let me get this straight. You want to be stupid. And you don't mind if I'm a liar."

Xander blinked at him. "No . . . I . . . Keal, I thought you and I kind of understood each other."

"How so?"

Xander looked to David, saw nothing that would help him. "You know, you're all about going for it. Whatever it takes. Get it done."

Keal leveled a steely gaze at Xander. "You misunderstand me."

Xander crossed his arms. He pushed his shoulder into the wall and said, "Enlighten me."

David closed his eyes. Sometimes it seemed that Xander enjoyed being difficult.

Keal plopped down on the bench. "Okay," he said. "It's not about just *doing*. It's about doing it right. A man has to feed his family, but if he does it by robbing and stealing, he's not doing it right. A man's nothing without integrity."

"Wait a minute," Xander said. "You snuck into the hospital to see Jesse. And didn't you tell us that you chased away the cops who were watching the house the other night? You threw rocks at their car!"

Keal nodded. "It's not always easy, trying to do the right thing. Sometimes we blow it. And sometimes you bend the rules for a greater good. Jesse believed you were in danger in this house. We had to get in to see you without being detained." He stared up at the light, thinking. "Put it this way: Would I punch a cop for no good reason? No. Would I punch him because he was writing me a ticket or taking me to jail for doing something wrong? No. On the other hand, if he was keeping me from saving someone's life, and he wouldn't listen to reason . . ." Keal shrugged. "Yeah, I'd punch him. Then I'd save the life and face the consequences of my actions. But not everyone thinks that way."

David made a face. He said, "There are people who'd let the person die?"

"If saving him meant breaking rules or hurting someone, yeah."

"But," David said, "getting punched in the face is nothing compared to *dying*."

Xander threw up his hands. "That's what I'm talking about, Keal. I'm trying to save Mom. That's more important than following Dad's rules."

"But your dad wants to save her too," Keal said. "He *will* listen to reason. If he disagrees with what you want to do, it's probably based on sound judgment. There's your way, and there's his way. It's only a matter of opinion which way is better."

"But—" Xander started.

Keal stopped him with a raised hand. "You can't say for

certain that your way will rescue your mother faster than his way."

"My way is *doing*," Xander said. "Make it happen."

"Or die," Keal said. "His way is to prepare, be safe . . . and then do. It may not be as exciting, but it makes sense. In the end, Xander, you obey because he is your dad."

David rubbed his cast. His arm ached from getting banged around and from the snake bracelet's tugging toward the portal. He worked the bracelet off and set it on the bench beside him. He crossed one leg over the other and began untying the slippers.

Keal picked up the bracelet and turned it over in his hands. "So, why here, anyway? What made you go over?"

David dropped the shoe on the bench and lifted the other foot. He said, "Xander thought it was the world Jesse tried telling us about."

"A snake bracelet?" Keal said.

"The helmet," Xander said. "And look." He took the pouch off his belt and showed Keal the medallion with the house.

"But an ax?" Keal said. "Jesse wouldn't send you someplace you needed that."

David nodded. "That's what I said."

"Besides," Keal said, "I found the antechamber with Jesse's items."

thirty-seven

THURSDAY, 7:38 A.M.

"You found it?" Xander said. "Are you sure?"

"Pretty sure," Keal said.

"Where?"

"Few doors down," Keal said. "I looked while I was waiting for you. It's the freakiest thing, how the rooms change, the items in them. I hit each door three times, and every time there were different things inside."

"Right!" Xander said, opening the hallway door. "That's why you can't leave when you find the world you want." He went into the hallway. "Which one? It's probably gone."

Keal followed him out. David grabbed his sneakers and went into the hall. The antechamber door clicked shut behind him.

"Look," Keal said, pointing. "I blocked the door open with one of the little tables."

"That doesn't always work," Xander said, rushing to it. "Only a living person in the antechamber or through the portal can keep the room from changing." He slipped past the table into the room.

"Sounds like you're figuring this stuff out," Keal said. He looked back at David. "Coming?"

"Just a sec." David opened the door of the antechamber they just left. The slippers were gone, along with the rest of the Viking world items. Among the items in their place were an ornately colored robe—a *kimono*; a fan—the kind women flutter at their faces; and a long, curved sword—a *katana*, he thought it was called.

Cool, he thought. Then he imagined a bunch of ninjas coming at him with throwing stars, nunchucks, and swords, and he changed his mind. *Not going to get me into that world.*

He shut the door and went to Keal, who had pulled the table out of the way. David slipped past him into the antechamber.

Xander was smiling. "I think he's right." He held up a claw hammer.

David scanned the items hanging on the hooks. "What about the buck teeth?"

"Check it out." Xander set the hammer down and grabbed a utility belt. He held it over his waist. Two rectangular leather pouches hung down, one over each leg.

David marveled at how similar it was to Jesse's drawing. He said, "For holding nails and stuff, like the one Dad has. What about the house?"

The boys looked at the other items on the bench and hooks: a saw; a metal bulb with a pointed tip, hanging by a string—a plumb bob; and a tool David thought was used to sort of file down wood—a plane or planer, something like that. Nothing that resembled a house.

Xander scratched his head. "Maybe we're supposed to *infer* a house, because these are home-building tools."

"No, no," Keal said, stepping up to the bench. "It's hard to see." He scooted aside the planer thing, picked up a scrap of paper, and held it up.

"It's the corner of a blueprint," David said. It showed the corner of a building, a room, and stairs.

"That's it?" Xander said. "Just a torn piece of paper?"

"It's a house," David said. "Home builders use blueprints. I'm sold."

Xander took the paper from Keal, examined it, nodded. He turned and looked at the portal door. Over his shoulder, he said, "Well, what do you think?"

"What do you mean, what do I think?" David said. "Go over? Now? We just came back. I'm beat—again."

"You didn't get hurt," Xander said. "That was a horrible one, but we got out better than we usually do. You said yourself you think this is the one. The one Jesse—"

"Whoa," Keal said. "I promised your dad I'd bring you to school."

"Keal," Xander said, a little whiny, "Jesse wanted us to find this place. If we leave now, it may not come back for a long time, if ever. We can't just *ignore* it. Jesse thinks—"

"Hold on," Keal said. He scratched his chin. "I'm sure it is important, but—"

"You want to sit in here and hold it till we come home?" Xander said. "Don't you have other things you wanted to do? You won't be able to go the bathroom or—"

"I'll manage," Keal said.

Xander started to say something else, but Keal stopped him. "Give me a minute. I'm thinking." His eyes roamed over the items, then settled on David. "Okay, okay. Let's call your dad."

"What?" Xander complained. "He'll just say—"

"That's the way it is, Xander," Keal said. "Take it or leave it."

Xander frowned. He waved his hand toward the hallway door. "Fine, go call him."

Keal smiled and shook his head. He made a come-here

gesture with his finger. "You're coming with me. David, you stay. If you hear anything that's not us, run. Forget about the room and get your butt downstairs, understand?"

David nodded. "But who's going over . . . if we do?"

"I am," Xander said.

"That means both of us," David said with a sigh. "I'm sticking with you. Jesse said—"

"I know, I know, stay together."

"What about Keal?" David said. "He could go."

"I think *you* should go," Keal said. "I'm pretty sure the message was for you guys. With Jesse, it's always been about you. Where's Xander's phone?"

"On the floor in the hall downstairs," David said.

"Come on, then," Xander said. He brushed past Keal and left the antechamber.

"You going to be all right?" Keal asked David.

"If I hear so much as a rat's fart, I'm outta here."

Keal grinned. "What about going over? You cool with that?"

He nodded. "I'm tired, but it's important to Jesse."

After Keal left, David began psyching himself up. He stood, stretched, made sure the Ace bandages over his cast were tight. He put on his sneakers and tied them tightly. He looked at the items. Not a weapon among them. He liked that. Then again, there wasn't a weapon in the future world antechamber, either. And except for the machete, none for the jungle world; even so, he had been almost eaten by tigers and skewered by warriors. He rubbed his shoulder where the arrow had nicked him.

I can do this, he thought.

Mom had a saying for every situation. Most of them didn't make a lot of sense to David: dollars to doughnuts (*what?*), a lost ball in high weeds (*had something to do with not knowing what you were doing—come on!*), don't add insult to injury (*okay, I sort of get that one*). The one that came to mind now was, "In for a penny, in for a pound." Obviously, from England; a pound was like the American dollar. It meant if something was worth doing at all, it was worth doing right—committing yourself to doing it all the way. When it came to rescuing Mom, he was in for a penny, in for a pound. Going over was part of that.

Xander was right. He had no new injuries. So why not go into another world now?

He heard something and jumped. Someone was pounding up the stairs, fast.

Xander better not be running to go over, despite being told no, David thought. *I can hold him back at least until Keal comes.*

He went to the hallway entrance. He held on to the frame so the door couldn't slam and knock him into the hall—you never knew about this place. And that might cause them to lose their chance to discover what it was Jesse wanted them to find.

Xander hit the landing and darted into the hallway. He was smiling. "Dad said yes. You should have heard Keal. He was great. He said to find Mom, we're going to have to do things, like just us going over sometimes." He pushed past David into the room.

"That doesn't mean whenever you want," David said.

"I know. Don't be such a baby."

"I'm not a—" He stopped. There was no arguing with Xander sometimes. David could fight a thousand wars, rescue children from burning buildings, stay in this house alone, and Xander would still find a reason to call him a baby.

Keal stepped into the doorway. "Xander, only take enough items to open the door," he said. "Both of you go together. When you get there, give an item to David, so he can get back if you get separated. That way, I'll be able to come get you, if you're not back in—" He looked at his watch. "Say, a half hour. Deal?"

"What if it takes longer?" Xander said. "What if—"

"Half an hour," Keal repeated. "That's it. Don't make me come drag you home. What?" He was looking at David's grin.

"Mom would like you," David said.

He patted David on the arm. "I'm sure I'd like her too." He pointed. "Take the hammer, tool belt, and blueprint. Those are the things Jesse specified. Better stick to the plan."

Xander strapped on the tool belt and picked up the hammer and scrap of paper. He opened the portal door. Bright sunlight streamed in. A fresh smell, like trees and grass, blew in on a gentle breeze.

"What do you see?" David said.

"Trees." Xander smiled over his shoulder. "Nothing but trees. Ready?"

David returned the smile. "Let's do it."

thirty-eight

Xander had been right: nothing but trees in every direction. David couldn't name them to save his life, but he appreciated their beauty. Sunbeams speared down from the sky, breaking through the foliage in a hundred places. So while much of the woods was in shadow, it wasn't spooky. A warm breeze touched his arms and face. It was the kind of place the King family used to go for picnics. They'd always favored the woods over parks and open areas. Maybe that's one reason they'd liked the house when they'd first found it.

Should've kept looking, he thought. But even if they'd hated it, Dad would have insisted. That'd been his plan.

David sat on the ground where he had wound up after spilling out from the portal. He had tucked his cast close to his body and avoided getting it banged again. Maybe he was starting to figure out this portal-jumping business.

Xander hadn't been as lucky. He had cracked his head on a tree, and now he was sitting up against it, rubbing his skull.

David stood. "You okay?"

"My head's getting more knots than these trees," Xander said. "Here." He held the scrap of blueprint.

David took it and flapped it around. "This little thing has a pull I'd be able to feel?"

"Drop it and follow it, like we did the yarn. Just don't lose sight of it."

David pushed it into his back pocket. He looked around. "Any idea where we should go?"

Xander pushed himself up. "Just start walking, I guess."

They'd gone forty or fifty paces when a sound reached them. It was the distinctive *pound-pound-pound* of a hammer. Someone pounded, paused, pounded. David could almost see him hammering in a nail, lining up another one, and pounding on it.

Xander raised his eyebrows, and the brothers headed for the sound.

The pounding continued, grew louder, then stopped.

They trudged on, going around bushes, ducking under branches.

Xander braked. His arm shot up to stop David. "No way!"

David followed his gaze, and his heart skipped a beat. Carved into a tree was the face of their family mascot, Bob. David ran to it. He put his fingertip into the groove that made Bob's bulbous chin. "Looks fresh," he said.

Xander stepped beside him. He brushed his fingers over the whole face.

"You think it's Mom?" David said. Hoping against hope.

"Who else?" Xander said, smiling.

David had seen it on the *Titanic* too. "She could be leaving messages for us," he said, "like we are for her. Telling us where she's been."

"Maybe it's like a marker," Xander said. "You know, not just where she's been, but a place to go. If she finds herself in a world she's already been to, she comes to where she left Bob and waits. If we do the same, we'll have a better chance of finding each other."

"Maybe she's here," David said. "Now."

"Could Jesse have known that?" Xander puzzled.

The pounding started again.

"Come on," David said, heading toward the sound. As he walked, he scanned everywhere, looking for more signs, a person, Mom.

They went up a small incline, then down the other side till

they came to a wall of bushes that stretched a good distance on either side. Xander pushed through, and David followed. When he emerged, he bumped into Xander's outstretched arm.

Xander was staring at someone sitting on a log fifty feet away. The person's back was to them. He—David thought it was a he—was wearing a white T-shirt and blue jeans. Nothing weird, like the other worlds they'd visited. He had blond hair, and his head was bent forward. The way his shoulders and arms moved, he was fiddling with something, David thought. Not just sitting there or reading a book.

Xander started for him, tiptoeing.

David caught up and tapped him. He whispered, "Shouldn't we call to him? We don't want to scare him."

"I want to make sure that's not a gun he's got, first," Xander said. He took a step. A twig snapped under his foot.

The person snapped his head around. He set something on the ground, hopped up, and turned. He was a boy, about David's age. He stared at them, his mouth hanging open. David saw that he was gripping a knife.

David waved. "Hi! We didn't mean to scare you."

"Does he even speak English?" Xander whispered.

"What are you doing here?" the boy said.

David backhanded Xander's leg. "We're looking for someone."

"Who?" The boy looked in the direction of the hammering.

"Our mother," David said.

"You lost her? Around here?"

David walked toward him. "It's sort of hard to explain."

The boy took a step back. His foot came down on something, and he almost fell. "Stay there!" he said. He lifted the knife, but he didn't look like someone who'd use it on them.

David stopped. "We're not here to hurt you. We want to just look around."

"Well, you can't. Not here. This is private property. You're trespassing."

"Come on, man!" Xander said. He strode past David.

"Dad!" the boy yelled toward the pounding. "Dad!" The hammering continued.

David fell in beside Xander. When they were twenty feet from the kid, they stopped. Xander lifted his arm over David's head, pointing. "There's a face on a tree over there, a cartoon face. Do you know anything about it?"

"What's it to you?"

"Like my brother said, we're just looking for someone. You don't have to cop an attitude, all right?"

The boy looked puzzled.

"The face?" David said.

"I carved it," the boy said.

"*You* did?" Xander said. "Where did you—"

"What year is it?" the boy demanded.

Xander squinted at him. "What?"

"What year is it!" He screamed it.

The pounding stopped, then resumed.

David and Xander looked at each other. David shrugged.

"Uh . . ." Xander said.

"I knew it!" the boy said, stepping back. "I knew it! *Dad! Dad!* You have to go back! You don't belong here!"

"Wait a minute," Xander said, walking forward. "You know about the . . . the . . ."

The boy backpedaled and went down on his butt.

Xander stepped over the log.

The boy pointed the knife at him. "Stay back!"

"Xander," David said, stepping over the log. "You're scaring him."

"He knows, Dae. He knows about the portals."

"Portals?" the boy said. "What are portals?"

David shifted his feet. His heel tapped something that rustled. A brown paper sack, its top rolled tight. His eyes shifted to the thing the kid had been fiddling with before they startled him. He stopped breathing.

It was a box, shaped like a half cylinder. Carved into its curving surface was a warrior thrusting a spear. The warrior's target was smooth wood, but David knew what would go there: another fighter. He'd seen it before, finished. And it wasn't a box. It was one of the wall lights in the curvy third-floor hallway of their house.

"You . . ." David said. He looked at the boy, who was

looking up at him with big blue eyes. "Who are you? I'm David. This is my brother, Xander. What's your name?"

Before the boy answered, David knew. Those blue-blue eyes.

The boy's brows came together. He said, "I'm Jesse. Jesse King."

CHAPTER

thirty-nine

David sat down hard on the log.

"What?" Xander said.

David grinned. He waved his hand at the boy. "Xander, he's Jesse! *Jesse!*"

Xander's face swung around to the boy, then back to David. "That's not Jesse's last name. It's . . . it's . . ."

"*Wagner,*" David said. "He *changed* it! He told me! He said a lot of people in our family go by different last names. Because of . . . I don't know, the house or what they do or something, they change their names."

Xander appeared completely baffled. He leaned closer to the boy, squinted at him. "Jesse?"

"That's my name," the boy said. "But . . . but I don't know you. What is he talking about?"

"Look at his eyes, Xander," David said. "Don't you recognize them? This is how he knew you and me, but not Toria. Remember? When we first met him, he knew our names. You asked how he knew us, and he said something like, 'Well, *I've* met *you*.' It was weird, because I thought, how do you meet someone but they don't meet you? He *had* met us—when he was a kid. He remembered. But at the time, we hadn't met him."

Xander nodded, but his face still held on to a puzzled expression. "This is too weird."

"What are you guys talking about?" Jesse said.

David said, "You know about the portals, right?"

Jesse simply stared at him.

"Maybe you don't call them that," David said. "The time traveling? Going to different times and places?"

Jesse looked at each of them in turn. He scrambled up. "I have to go get my father."

"Wait," David said. "We're Kings too. If you know about the time traveling, then maybe you'll believe this. We come from the future."

Xander laughed. "Oh, man, that's a line."

David smiled, but continued. "You're our great-great-uncle." He could've said "We're from Mars" and not have gotten a more confused-worried-startled look from Jesse. "I know it sounds crazy. Look, how old are you—like, twelve?"

"Fourteen."

"Fourteen? Well, you look younger than your years when you're ninety too."

Xander was looking at David, a half smile showing his amusement.

"So." David put his fingers to his temple and calculated. "Then it's . . . 1929! Right?"

"Thirty-one."

David waved his hand in front of himself. "I don't know Jesse's exact age. Ninety something. But I was close."

Jesse looked toward the pounding, then back to David.

"Okay, see this?" David bent and picked up the wall light.

Xander saw it, and said, "Whoa! That's—"

"Shhh," David said. "Don't say anything."

Jesse stepped forward. "Hey, put that down."

"Dude!" Xander told him, holding his palms out. "Get rid of the knife, all right?"

Jesse looked at it as though he'd forgotten about it. He said, "What about *that*?" He nodded toward the hammer in Xander's hand.

Xander hooked the claw onto his back pocket.

Jesse folded the knife blade into the handle and pushed it into his front pocket.

"Okay," David said. He held up the wall light as though he were displaying it to his class for show-and-tell. "See this blank area where you haven't carved anything yet?"

Jesse nodded.

"It's going to be another warrior. He's getting stabbed by this guy's spear." He smiled at Jesse.

Jesse's mouth dropped open. His eyes went wide, and he stared at David. "How did you . . . ? Let me see that." He grabbed the wall light and squinted at the blank area.

"And," David said, "I don't know if you even know this yet, but you—or somebody—is going to carve all the way through. You're going to make slits in the eyes, along the spear, in a kind of sunshiny pattern above the stabbed guy."

"Yeah," Jesse said. "I was planning to do that."

"Because it's a wall light, right?"

Jesse handed the carving back to David. His legs folded, and he sat on the ground. He looked at David, really looked at him. He did the same with Xander. He said, "So you guys came through the holes?"

"You sent us," David said.

"Me?"

"When you're an old man. You come to help us, but . . ."

"But what?"

"Nothing." David caught Xander's eye.

His brother shook his head, clearly sharing David's thought: *He doesn't need to know he gets stabbed.*

"So you know me as an old man?"

"Yeah," David said. "You got a long life ahead of you."

Jesse smiled. "Am I hip?"

"Hip?" David said. "Oh, you mean cool. Yeah, you're totally hip."

"You're a good guy," Xander agreed.

David shifted his foot, and it came down on the brown paper sack. He felt something squish inside.

Jesse leaned over and snatched it up. He opened it, then pulled out a sandwich, half flattened.

"Sorry," David said.

Jesse smiled and held it out to him. "Hungry?"

"No, thanks."

Xander shook his head.

Jesse produced a piece of hard candy in a wrapper. He tossed it to David, and a second one to Xander. David set his down and shook his head at Xander.

"So," David said. He picked up the wall light. "Why are you making this?"

"Don't you know?" Jesse said. "Didn't I tell you?"

David frowned. "We haven't known the old Jesse that long. Just a few days."

"But you said I'm your great—"

"Great-great uncle," David said. "But we didn't know you even existed until a few days ago."

"That's too bad," Jesse said. "Maybe I'll come find you sooner now . . . after you're born." He smiled, and David's heart ached: he recognized it.

"I don't think so," Xander said. "We already know that part of our past."

"But that's okay," David said. "You come when we need you."

CHAPTER

forty

Jesse pointed at the wall light. "Sometimes people come through the holes. Dad thinks they *stumble* into them the first time, you know, by accident."

"The first time?" Xander said.

"Sometimes they come back," Jesse said. "They figure out where the holes are in their time. Maybe they mark them or something. Maybe they don't move around the way they do when Dad goes into one and has to come back."

"Your father goes over?" Xander said.

"Oh, yeah. That's what we do."

"*We?* You go?"

Jesse's face grew long. "Not yet. Dad says I'm too young. But someday. How old are *you?*"

"Fifteen," Xander said.

"Twelve," David said.

"Wow," Jesse said. "Your dad must be hip."

"He is," David said. "What about the wall light?" He was starting to believe it was for this that Jesse wanted them to find him. Then it dawned on him: this was what he meant when he said "Come see me."

"Well," Jesse said, "we don't know how, but the people find their way back here."

"Why?" Xander said. "What do they do?"

"Explore, I guess," Jesse said. "They usually come back armed. Spears, knives, clubs. Dad says they're just mean-spirited and looking for trouble."

"Then what?" Xander said.

"Usually we catch them, hold them till we find the hole they came from. Sometimes we have to wait until we feel the hole looking for them."

"The *pull*," David said.

"Yeah, like that," Jesse said. "Then we throw them back in."

"You *throw* them back into the portal . . . the hole? You and your dad?"

"Mostly Dad and my older brother, Aaron."

"Hold on," Xander said. "Doesn't the door stay open till they go back?" He looked at David. "It does when Phemus comes through."

"Door?"

"The door over the port . . . the hole. You know, through the antechamber."

"Ante-what?"

"The little room where the portal door is."

Jesse's face lit up. "You go through a door? And there's a little room for each door?"

"Yeah," Xander said. "Don't you?"

"Not yet," Jesse said, excited. "Dad's building them now! He put one together just to see if his idea worked. It did, so we're building a bunch of them. And a house that we're going to live in!"

"You're building the house?" Xander said. "Now?"

Jesse touched his ear and held his finger up, indicating the pounding. "That's what he's doing."

Xander looked that direction. "Oh, this I gotta see."

"Jesse," David said, hefting the wall light. "You were going to tell us about this?"

"Right," Jesse said. "Like I said, *usually* we catch them. Sometimes they get away or we never know they came through. One started coming regular. He'd go into town, steal stuff. Killed some people too. Dad went after him, ended up going over to his time, some ancient civilization. Dad realized there were a lot of superstitions back then, some things that scared the bejeepers out of people. So he made a little statue of some deity they were really afraid of. He put it in the area where that guy was coming through, and he stopped coming."

"So they're like talismans," Xander said. "Magic symbols that keep evil away."

"But it's not magic," Jesse said. He smiled. "We're just using their own superstitions against them. We've done it for *eight* people-groups now. Works every time, so far. We're going to put them in the hallway, where the holes are."

David stood. He handed the wall light to Jesse. "So, you figure out what scares them, what their superstitions are, and make a light."

"Yep." Jesse got up. "Want to see the house?"

"Yes!" Xander said.

"But we can't," David said. "We have to get back. I think we're already late."

"Dae," Xander said, "if Dad and Keal knew how much we could learn here . . ."

"I don't think it's our choice," David said. He pointed at the hammer hooked to Xander's pocket. The handle was pointing straight back, quivering in the direction they had come.

Xander grabbed it before it could fly away.

"If we try to stay, we might lose the items," David said. "Or they'll drag us back kicking and screaming."

He pulled the corner of blueprint out of his pocket and held it up. It bent over his thumbnail and fluttered, as though in a strong wind. It confirmed the hammer's directive.

"Hey," Jesse said, pointing at the paper. "Where'd you get that?"

"It was in the antechamber," David said. "In the small room with the hole that brought us here."

Jesse smiled and shook his head. "Dad looked all over for it. That corner got stuck on a board when he grabbed the blueprints a couple weeks ago. When he moved the board to get it, it blew away."

"This is the blueprint for our house?" David said.

"Mine now, yours later."

"Much later," Xander said. "Next time we come, you can show us the house."

"You'll be back?" Jesse said, like a kid heading to Disneyland.

David understood; he'd felt it when he first met old Jesse: the chance to share a secret with someone who cared, someone who really got it.

Jesse extended his hand to Xander. "Until then, great-great-nephew."

Xander shook his hand.

Jesse held out his hand to David, who glanced at it and then up to the boy's face. He didn't see some kid he'd just met; he saw Jesse, the Jesse he knew and loved and had cried for that very morning. Fourteen or ninety-something—he was still Jesse. David brushed aside Jesse's hand, stepped in, and hugged him. He squeezed him tightly, then took a step back.

Jesse offered him an awkward smile, and David felt his face flush. He said, "I'm . . . just glad you sent us to find you."

Xander tossed the hammer. When he went after it, stooping low to grab it, David realized he hadn't tossed it; it had flown out of his hand. Xander crashed into the wall of bushes and disappeared.

"Gotta go," David said. "Take care of yourself."

"I guess I do," Jesse said.

David ran after Xander.

CHAPTER

forty-one

THURSDAY, 8:30 A.M.

David lay sprawled on the antechamber floor. Xander sat next to him, breathing heavily.

The portal door slammed shut.

Keal leaned over David, casting a shadow over him like an angry god. "You're five minutes late," he said, his voice rumbling. He was holding the planer and saw.

"That was incredible," David said.

"Guess who we met?" Xander said.

"How would I know? The guy who built the Taj Mahal? What's his name, Shah Jahan?"

"How do you even know that?" David said.

Xander said, "Try the guy who built this house."

"The guy who—" Keal gaped at them. "You saw Jesse?"

"At fourteen," David said. "But he looked twelve."

"Fourteen?" Keal said. "Years old?"

Xander nodded. "He was pretty cool."

"Hip," David corrected.

"Right, hip. Just like now."

"Wait, wait, wait," Keal said. "Are you guys punking me? You're kidding, right?"

"Keal," David said, "that's what he meant when he said, 'Come see me.' He didn't mean at the hospital. He meant back then. He remembered that we *did* go see him when he was a kid."

"Maybe if we didn't go," Xander said, "it would have changed things. He wanted to make sure we did what he knew we had to do."

"Did you save his life or something?" Keal said.

"No, but he may have saved ours," David said.

"What, just now?" Judging by the rising tone of his voice, Keal was growing more confused by the second.

David laughed. "He told us how to keep Phemus out of the house."

"What? Really? How?" Keal dropped down onto the bench.

"Scare him," Xander said.

"Oh," Keal said. "Yeah, why didn't I think of that? I got a Casper the Ghost mask in the car."

"Really," David said. "We need to find out what superstitions he believes and make a wall light."

"What, like the ones in the hallway?"

"Exactly," David said. "Jesse was making one when we met him just now."

"Jesse made them?"

"At least some of them," Xander said. He spun around to face Keal directly. "We need to go back. There's so much he can teach us. They were building the house, but we didn't have time to see it. Can you imagine all they must know, Jesse, his dad, and his brother?"

"Not today, Xander," Keal said. He looked at his watch. "School. No ifs, ands, or buts."

"But," Xander said.

"If," David said.

"And," Xander finished.

"I'm glad you guys are feeling better." Keal stood and opened the hallway door. "Let's go."

David groaned. "Isn't school almost over?"

"Barely started," Keal said. "It's only eight thirty."

David groaned again. "It feels like late afternoon. It was dark at the hospital. I got the sense it was early evening in the

Viking world. And Jesse offered us his lunch. These portals mess with your mind."

"Your biorhythms," Keal said. "Your body clock. Extreme jet lag."

"Whatever you call it," David said, "I don't like it."

"Plus everything else," Xander said. "What we do in the worlds: run, fight, get scared to death every two minutes. Then every time I go through a portal, I feel like I did an hour of exercise. How about a nap, just a short one?"

"Nope," Keal said.

The wind blew in from under the door. It scrubbed the boys of dirt and leaves that belonged back in young Jesse's time.

"Whoa," Xander said. He swiveled on the floor and slid into the portal door, cracking his hip hard enough for David to hear it. He pushed away. Dropping onto his back, he planted his feet on the door and pushed. He spun sideways and flew into the door again.

David hopped up and grabbed one of Xander's ankles. Keal grabbed the other. They pulled his legs away from the door and backed toward the hallway. David could feel the pull on his brother. His pants were riding high now, as though they were going to rip apart and sail over his head.

"What do you have?" David said.

"I don't know!"

One of Xander's front pockets pulled out, poking from his jeans like a dog's ear. The candy Jesse had tossed him popped out, skidded across the floor, and jammed into the crack under the door. It crunched and broke and disappeared.

David and Keal dropped his legs.

"See?" David said.

Xander got up, tugging down on his pants. He shifted uncomfortably and grimaced at David. "Time just gave me a wedgie."

forty-two

THURSDAY, 11:55 A.M.

David sat in the cafeteria, staring down at his hot-lunch tray. The wedge of pizza was crusty, burned, and cold. He thought the goop in a paper cup was rice pudding. The salad looked okay, but he couldn't eat it. He was hungry, but the image of the berserker chowing down on that guy and the memory of that rancid breath in his face kept popping up every few minutes. He'd been doing a pretty good job of keeping his mind on meeting young Jesse and suppressing everything else: Jesse in the hospital, the destroyed future and the creatures from that time, the *Titanic* . . . *Mom!* But that berserker—man, that haunted him.

Between physical exhaustion and too many memories and emotions to manage, he wasn't worth anything today. He had made it to school in time for his second-period class, algebra, and then to Ancient Civilizations (was his taking *that* a cosmic joke or what?), but he couldn't remember one word the teachers had said. He had walked through the halls like a zombie.

He hoped it was the fatigue and stress making him this way. It had crossed his mind that next to everything he did at home and in the worlds, ordinary life was just plain boring. Then he reminded himself that living in a constant state of fear, having more than one brush with death a day, and his mother being kidnapped were not exciting. Adrenaline inducing? Yes. But fun? Not by a long shot.

All he wanted was Mom back.

Give us Mom back, he thought, *and I'll study hard, never miss a class, become an accountant or some other ho-hum guy, and never, ever complain about being bored. Promise.*

"David!"

He snapped his head up. "Huh?"

Ben, Marcus, and Anthony laughed.

"See?" Ben said. "He wasn't sleeping."

"You yelled in his ear," Marcus countered. "Were you sleeping, David?"

Anthony said, " 'Cause we've been talking to you for like ten minutes, and you didn't even nod your head."

"I think he groaned once," Ben said.

"I'm telling you," Marcus said, "that was a snore."

"Anthony said you wear girls' panties," Ben said.

They all laughed.

"Pink ones," Anthony said, snorting, "with pictures of Barbie dolls on them!"

"That's when we knew you were *out*," Marcus said.

"Not sleeping," Ben said. "Just out. The lights were on, but nobody was home."

"No, sleeping," Marcus said. "Right?" He pointed at the pizza. "Are you going to eat that?"

David handed it to him. "Sorry, guys," he said. "I'm just tired, and . . ." He wanted to offer something to explain. "And my uncle's in the hospital."

Ben said, "Oh, man."

"Is he all right?" Marcus said.

Anthony slapped Marcus's shoulder. "He's in the *hos-pi-tal!* What do you think?"

"I meant, is he *going* to be all right? David knew what I meant."

"Are you close?" Anthony asked David.

"He lives in Chicago," David said. Not a lie, exactly.

"No . . . *close*. Are you like friends, buddies?"

David smiled. "Yeah, I like him. A *lot*."

"What's he in for?" Ben said.

"That sounds like he's in prison," Marcus said.

"He got mugged," David said. *There it is: a lie. See what happens when you open your mouth?* "They beat him up pretty badly."

"Is he going to make it?" Anthony asked.

David shrugged. He looked down at the moldering rice pudding.

The guys mumbled among themselves. David didn't listen, and he didn't look up when they scraped their chairs back and picked up their trays. Someone tapped his arm. It was Anthony.

"Sorry about your uncle, man. So you're probably not up for some football, huh? We throw it around at lunch."

"Nah, not today. Thanks, though."

David watched them take their trays to the trash, dump them, and put them on a stack. He got up and did the same. In the hall, he turned toward his locker. Fourth period. What was it? For the life of him, he couldn't remember. Well, it was only the fourth day of classes. Even kids without David's level of extracurricular activity didn't memorize their schedule this quickly, right? Language arts! That was it. See? He was okay.

He went around a corner and found himself face-to-face with Clayton, the bully who'd followed him through locker

119 to the linen closet in their house. To keep him quiet, David had threatened him.

Clayton's skin color changed before David's eyes, as though all the blood in his head was draining out. Clayton lowered his head, spun around, and tromped off.

Wow, David thought. His threats hadn't been *that* awful, had they? He'd said he would post pictures of Clayton crying like a baby on the Internet and that he'd return him to the locker, where he couldn't escape. That one was kind of scary. Or maybe it was just that David's family lived in a freaky home that teleported people through space—that could be enough to make Clayton keep his distance. David had started thinking of the locker portal as no big thing, at least compared to what the third-floor rooms did. But it *was* big. Huge. That alone made the house special . . . *creepy*.

"Hey," David called. "Clayton!"

The kid walked faster. David hurried to catch up. Clayton turned into a classroom. David followed. It was empty, except for Clayton. He was standing behind the teacher's desk.

"Stay away from me," Clayton said.

Boy, had things changed.

"Look," David said. "About the other day . . ."

"Forget it," Clayton said. "There was no other day, okay? Nothing happened. Just . . . just leave me alone."

David felt sorry for him, sort of. He had never been a bully himself, and now he understood why. He didn't like putting this kind of fear in people. It made him feel small.

"I didn't mean to scare you," David said. "I'm sorry."

"Scare me?" Clayton laughed. "You? Don't flatter yourself."

"Then . . . what's this about? You running from me?"

"I just don't want anything to do with you or your freaky witch-house or your creepy friends! You're still a little punk, don't think you're not."

David nodded. He turned to leave, then stopped. He pushed the door closed and stepped closer to Clayton. "What creepy friends?"

"Just . . . all of them."

"Clayton," David said, "who are you talking about?"

"Get out of here," Clayton said. "Go on, get out of here. Let me alone."

"Did someone threaten you? Besides me, I mean."

"You call your little yips *threats*? You don't—"

"Clayton!" David slid into the desk seat beside him.

"What are you doing?" Clayton said.

"Talking."

"Not to me, you aren't. If you want to stay, fine." He started around the desk.

"Wait," David said. "Let me tell you something."

Clayton stopped. "What?" he said through gritted teeth.

"There's a man," David said. "His name is Taksidian."

Clayton's eyes widened. He turned his head toward the window.

Looking for something, David thought. *For someone.*

Clayton took a step back. "I don't know what you're talking about. I don't know any Taks-whatever."

"He's a really, really bad guy," David said. "The worst person ever. I think you know that. But, Clayton, he's not a friend of mine. He wants our house. He'll do anything to get it. He's hurt my family. He's hurt us bad."

Clayton blinked. His hard features softened, just a little.

"He's still hurting us. And he wants to hurt a lot of people. Not just my family."

Clayton examined his shoes. He said, "What's your point?"

"One: It's not me or my family you should stay away from, it's him. Hate us, if you want to. Never talk to me again, if it makes you feel better. But stay away from Taksidian. For your sake, stay away from him."

Clayton rocked between his left and right feet. He said, "What's number two?"

"Two." David cleared his throat. "If there's anything you can do to help us, if you know anything about him that will help us put him away, you'd be helping more than my family. You'd be helping more people than you can imagine. I'm not kidding. I know you don't like me. You want to pound me. I get that. But would it really make you happy if I died? If my whole family died? If a lot of people died?"

Guilt, shame—something like that—touched Clayton's face. He gave David a one-shoulder shrug. He whispered, "I don't want that."

"Please," David said. "If you can, help us."

Clayton studied the floor tiles. His eyes flashed up to David, then lowered again. They were silent for five, ten seconds—an eternity after that conversation. The wall clock ticked, ticked.

Keeping his gaze on the floor, Clayton walked for the door. As he passed David, he said, "I'll think about it."

David looked down at the desk. Kids had etched words into its surface: NICHOLAS . . . ALLISON+SCOTT . . . MR. REED STINKS. He heard the door open, then click shut.

If Clayton told anyone—his parents, cops—what David had said, would it cause trouble? He didn't think so. Even if he told Taksidian, what more harm could Taksidian do? He hoped that if nothing else, this would make Clayton stay away from Taksidian. Just as he knew Clayton didn't wish serious hurt on David, David didn't want him hurt either. And hurt was what Taksidian was all about.

CHAPTER

forty-three

THURSDAY, 3:07 P.M.

David closed his locker and saw Xander heading for him, weaving around kids. He pushed his backpack strap over his shoulder. "Xander, what's—?"

Xander grabbed his arm. He turned around and pulled David back the way he'd come. "Follow me." He released his grip.

"What's up?" David said.

Xander said nothing, just walked.

"Xander," David said. "What's going on?"

"He's here."

"Who?"

Xander stopped, turned, and whispered, "Taksidian."

David's throat tightened. "Where?" He looked up and down the hall, out the window that ran the length of the hall, opposite the lockers and classrooms. Cars were circling through the pickup lanes. People moving everywhere.

"Come on," Xander said. "He's been here awhile. I saw him before my last class."

They reached the end of the hall. Turning left would take them into another short corridor. It was the home of locker 119—the one that teleported people to the Kings' linen closet. Straight ahead were the double doors that opened into the cafeteria.

Xander grabbed David's arm again and led him to the corner, where the windows met the cafeteria wall.

"Okay," Xander said. "Look." He pointed, keeping his hand close to his chest.

"Where?"

The school was L-shaped. The administrative offices occupied the end of the shorter wing. Looking diagonally across the courtyard, David could see Dad's office windows. A driveway ran past the end of that wing to another parking lot behind the admin offices. Across the drive from the offices was another, smaller building. David thought the school used it for storage. It was also where the auto shop classes were held. It had a big roll-up door.

"Garage door," Xander said.

There he was, leaning against the door frame. The spot he'd chosen was shadowed from the sun. He was wearing that black slicker David remembered from all the other times he'd seen the man.

"Who stands outside a school like that?" David said. "Why aren't people chasing him away?"

"He's a friend of the town, remember?"

"You think he's waiting for us?" David said.

"He's not here for a PTA meeting."

"But why? He knows where we live."

"Maybe he's hoping to catch one of us alone," Xander said. "Or he's just spooking us."

"Okay, so we go home with Dad," David said. "If that's how he wants to spend his time, so what? He won't find us alone, and we already know he's a creepy bad guy."

"No, listen," Xander whispered. "Here's our chance."

"For what?"

"To find out something about *him*, to turn the tables."

"How?"

"We follow him," Xander said.

"To where?" David said. "He's probably going to follow Dad back home."

"What if he doesn't? What if he goes to *his* house? Then we'll know where he lives. What if he meets with someone? We'll get an idea of what he's up to."

"Yeah, and he could go grocery shopping, grab some fast food, get his car serviced—a hundred nothing things at a hundred nothing places."

"Cops follow people, Dae," Xander said. "Sometimes it pays off, sometimes it doesn't. You take your chances."

David let out a long breath. "So we're going to follow him to his car and then watch him drive off? We don't have wheels, Xander. Are we going to run?"

Xander jangled a set of keys in front of his face.

"What're those?" David said.

"Car keys."

"Whose?" David said. "How'd you get them?"

"A friend, okay. You ask too many questions."

"What friend? You don't have any friends here yet."

Xander rolled his eyes. "Dan. He's a school friend who wanted fifty bucks and a full tank of gas."

"And you're going to drive? Without a license? Again?"

"I thought we'd been over all this when I went to see Dad in jail and to the store for cameras," Xander said. "What's worse, a ticket . . . or *him*?"

David scanned the hallways. They'd cleared out fast. "What about Dad?" he said. "He'll want to take us right home."

"I'll go talk to him."

"And say what?"

"I'll think of something," Xander said. "You up for it?"

"I guess," David said. *In for a penny, in for a pound.*

"All right," Xander said. "Go out the back door, where the track is. Meet me in the student parking lot. It's on the side, over this way." He hitched his thumb at the cafeteria. "And don't let him see you."

CHAPTER

forty-four

There were more than a dozen cars in the lot, most of them
bangers. David guessed all but one of them belonged to the
athletes who were practicing their various sports on the track
and football field. The lot was situated down a short hill from
the school. He couldn't see the front courtyard or pickup lanes,
let alone the building by which Taksidian had been standing.

And that means he can't see me, David thought. Unless Taksidian

moved. But David believed he knew why the creep had posi-
tioned himself where he had: it was the only place where you
could see both the front entrance and the faculty parking lot
behind the offices. He wanted to spot the Kings regardless of
how they left the school.

Back door didn't cross your mind, did it?

A chill tingled the back of his neck. He rubbed it and
looked around, certain he would see Taksidian or one of his
goons. He'd be grinning and wiggling his fingers at David:
Hello . . . and gotcha! But he saw no one, only some athletes in
the distance.

And Xander. He was coming down the concrete steps from
the rear of the school to the parking lot. He jogged toward
David, sweeping his gaze over the cars as he did. He pointed
at one. "It's this one."

Xander was unlocking the driver's door of a VW Beetle—
not one of the cool new ones; this one was ancient, missing
most of its chrome trim, and appeared to have barely survived
a stint on the demolition derby circuit: Herbie the Love Bug
gone very, very bad. The parts that weren't rusted were painted
either washed-out baby blue or primer gray.

David said, "You paid fifty bucks to borrow this? You
could have bought it for that."

"I didn't pay to borrow the car," Xander said. "I paid to
find out more about Taksidian."

Behind Xander, a man was skipping down the concrete

steps from the school—fast. David jumped, realized it was Dad, and jumped again. "It's *Dad!*" he said.

"Yeah," Xander said. "He's tagging along."

"What? I thought—"

Xander shrugged. "By the time I got to his office, I had a long story all worked out. Then I saw him . . . something about how tired he looked, worn-out. He's aged five years in a week. I decided I couldn't lie to him."

David narrowed his eyes.

"Not *then*, anyway," Xander said. He flashed a big grin. "I told him the plan, and he said, 'When do we go?'"

"What about Toria?" David said.

"Keal's picking her up. Dad called her school, made sure it was cool."

Speaking of cool, David thought, watching Dad trot over to them.

Dad smiled at David. To Xander, he said, "Is he still there?"

"I think so," Xander said.

Dad held out his hand. "Keys?"

Xander looked injured. He said, "I got my permit. It's legal, with you in the car."

"You're right." Dad held up a finger. "But can you drive a strange car safely *and* tail somebody without being seen? All at the same time?"

Doubt crinkled Xander's brow, but he said, "Sure. We'll switch if I have trouble."

"Okay," Dad said.

Xander dropped into the driver's seat. As Dad came around the rear of the car, he gave David a what-have-I-done? face.

David opened the passenger door. A smell like gym socks and old French fries wafted out at him. He reeled back, waving his hand under his nose. "What is *that?*"

"Ah," Dad said, leaning in. "The smell of a teenager's car." He pulled the seat-back forward and stepped aside for David.

"There's no room for me," David said. He was staring at a backseat loaded down with empty soda cans, potato chip bags, homework papers, crumpled fast-food bags, a crusty T-shirt, and at least six loose rolls of toilet paper.

Disgusted, David pushed the trash away. By the time he could make out the disintegrating yellow foam of the seat cushion—no covering—the pile on the far side of the seat was bigger than he was. He stepped in and sat down slowly, careful not to cause an avalanche.

Dad pushed David's backpack into the front footwell. He said, "I'm going to have a look." He closed the door and ran to a grassy incline by the lot's entrance. He lay down and climbed the hill on elbows and knees.

"Like a pro," David said. "What if we found out Dad's really an international spy, like in *Spy Kids?*"

Xander looked over his shoulder at him. "Really?"

Dad raised his head and looked around, reminding David

of a meerkat show on Animal Planet. It was clear he hadn't spotted Taksidian.

"Oh, no," Xander said. "He must've left."

Dad's head swiveled slowly, then he jerked it down.

"Found him," David interpreted.

After holding his position for a while, Dad gestured for Xander to pull forward.

David said, "If this thing smokes"—and how could it not?—"we may as well go tell Taksidian we're tailing him."

Xander cranked the key. The Bug purred to life, a fast, deep-throated rumble.

David nodded appreciatively.

"Yeah," Xander said. "Dan knows what's important." He put it in gear and pulled up to the sloping drive.

Dad crouched low and hurried over. He plopped in, pulled the door shut. He said, "He's walking down the street."

"Great," David said. "He's the one on foot, and we're driving. That won't be obvious."

"This town is pretty spread out," Dad said. "He needs a car. Let's follow and see."

Xander said, "Fasten your seat belts. It's going to be a bumpy night."

"Bette Davis," Dad said. "*All About Eve.*"

Xander smiled at him. "There's hope for you yet."

"Please," David said, coughing, "could you roll down the windows?"

CHAPTER

forty-five

THURSDAY, 3:54 P.M.

Dad was out of the car again. He stood on the shoulder of the street that led away from the school. After sloping down a long hill, it banked left, where it became a frontage road beside Pinedale's Main Street. David and Xander waited in the car at the top of the hill.

Dad signaled to them: *Come. Hurry.*

Xander popped the clutch. The tires chirped, the Bug

sprang forward, and David jerked back. The top foot of trash next to him tumbled into his lap. He slapped it away.

Dad climbed in. "There," he said. "That Mercedes."

A black sedan drove away from them on the frontage road. It signaled to make a turn, which would bring it to Main Street.

"It was at the fire station," Dad said.

"Why?" David said. "Why didn't he park at the school?"

"I can't figure that guy out," Dad said. "And maybe that's part of it. It serves him well to be creepy and mysterious. All the easier to scare people into doing what he wants. Maybe he thinks appearing at his destination on foot adds something to his aura of mystery."

"Or he doesn't want people messing with his car," Xander said. "You know, disabling it, so he can't follow them."

"I know," David said. "If he commits a crime, his car won't be reported as having been in the area."

Dad nodded. "The only flaw in that sentence is the word *if.*"

Xander put to good use all the knowledge of tailing a suspect he'd learned from countless cop shows and movies. He kept his distance without losing sight of the Mercedes. He allowed other cars to pull in between them. He drove past the stores Taksidian pulled into, then circled back to wait among other parked cars.

Taksidian seemed to be going about the business of an

average guy doing average things. He stopped at the market and came out with a bag and a gallon of milk. He swung into the same drive-in diner where the Kings had ordered ice cream after the first day of school.

"I'm starving," David said, watching the servers carry trays of food out to the cars.

Xander said, "We're not picking up drive-through, if that's what you're thinking."

"Didn't you get lunch, Dae?" Dad asked.

"I did, but I didn't eat it."

Dad frowned back at him. "When we're done with this, we'll get something special."

While they watched Taksidian at the gas station, David started feeling uneasy. Something wasn't right. There was something familiar about all of this, a déjà vu feeling, but his mind wouldn't lock in on what it was.

Taksidian talked to the mechanic, who lifted the Mercedes' hood. A minute later, he slammed it down and rubbed his hands on a rag hanging from his belt. He nodded, shook Taksidian's hand, and vanished into the garage. Taksidian pulled out onto Main Street.

"Okay," Dad said. "He's heading out of town."

They passed the park rangers' headquarters on the right, the last true building in town. After that, only a few vegetable stands, souvenir shops, a bed-and-breakfast, and another gas station interrupted the parade of trees.

Xander said, "At least he's not heading to our house." Theirs was on the other side of town.

"National Forest land, up this way," Dad said.

The road became a series of endless curves. They caught glimpses of Taksidian's sedan only a couple times a minute. Xander would have had to practically hitch the Bug to the Mercedes to see him better.

"If he pulls off the road, we'll lose him," David said.

Dad said, "We can only do what we can do."

David said, "Whoa! I saw it through the trees. Around the next hairpin. I think he stopped."

Xander braked hard, and they all leaned into their shoulder belts.

David checked behind them. No cars.

"Go slowly," Dad instructed.

Xander navigated the Bug around a tight curve.

"Just ahead," David said. "It looked like it was pulled over. And I saw the brake lights."

They puttered along, looking into the fortresslike shield of trees.

Xander said, "If you're wrong, Dae, we'll never catch up."

David strained his eyes to penetrate the dark forest.

"Look there," Dad said. On the right, two ruts ran from the road into the trees.

"A service road?" Xander said. He pulled the Bug to the

shoulder directly over the ruts. Grass grew on either side and between them. Trees crowded in tight.

"Hardly wide enough for a car to pass," Dad said.

"I'll bet Taksidian likes it that way," David observed.

Xander reversed, shifted gears, and pulled the car's tires into the ruts. Shadows enfolded them like a black fist as they broke the sanctity of the forest.

"Like all those movies," Xander said, "where the unsuspecting campers trudge into the wilderness, never to be seen again." He glanced back at David, a sly grin on his face.

David didn't see anything to smile about.

CHAPTER

forty-six

THURSDAY, 4:43 P.M.

The Bug shook them like dice in a cup. The ruts led them up hills, down into streambeds, around boulders the size of houses. After about five minutes, Xander nosed around a bend and braked. The ruts ran straight to a clearing. The trees leading to it prevented David from seeing more than one corner of a house. The black sedan squatted out front like a guard dog.

Dad opened his door. "I'll find a place to pull out of sight."

David put his hand on Dad's shoulder. He said, "We know where he lives now. Let's go home."

"We don't know he lives here," Xander said.

Dad winked at David. "Let's snoop a little more, huh, Dae?"

David nodded. After all, his own home wasn't exactly a bastion of security.

Dad moved off, and Xander rolled the car back a few feet.

"Do you *think* he lives here?" David said.

"It's big-time Taksidianish," Xander said. "We've come this far. May as well be sure."

Dad opened the door. "Back ten yards. We can get it completely off the road and cover it up."

•••••••••

David, Dad, and Xander lay on pine needles and peat and watched the house. The forest here was even heavier than it was around their house. The sun was a lonely stranger to the forest floor, as evidenced by the damp sponginess, mushrooms, and strange, ground-hugging plants. David felt the earth's coldness through his shirt and pants.

They were behind bushes so thick that to see the house, they had to part the leaves with both hands.

"It looks more ordinary than I expected," David whispered. And it was: a standard brick ranch, with a bay window to the left of the front door and a cement porch. To the right of the door, between it and a single garage door, was a place where a smaller window once looked out onto the small front yard; it had been covered with bricks that didn't quite match the rest of the house.

Dad said, "Probably an old residence for a forest worker or game warden."

"Or it was built to only *look* that way," Xander said.

"Why build something so small and ugly if you can afford better?" David said, keeping his eyes on the place.

"Deception," Xander said. "The more ordinary and mundane, the easier it is for bad guys to move around unnoticed."

"I thought Taksidian *tried* to be creepy and mysterious."

"Slippery," Dad said. "Hard to pin down, to figure out. I think that's more his style."

"Well," David said, "that's pretty creepy and mysterious."

The front door opened. David narrowed the gap in the leaves before him. A scene suddenly played out in his imagination: Taksidian stepping out onto the front stoop, raising a huge Arnold Schwarzenegger–type machine gun, laughing insanely, and opening fire on their position.

Instead, Taksidian bounded down the three steps and walked to his car. He was whistling some tune and tossing and catching his keys.

Just an Average Joe skipping off to terrorize children and snip off the fingers of old folks, David thought.

Freak.

The Mercedes engine roared. A dark-tinted window slid down, releasing a symphony of strange music: chanting vocals, banging drums, and plucky strings—played so loudly it hurt David's ears from across the yard. The car reversed, swung around, and peeled down the rutted drive.

Xander pushed back from the bush and rose to his knees. "Let's go," he said.

"Where?" David said.

Xander said, "Check out the house."

Simultaneously, Dad said, "Follow Taksidian."

"Follow him?" Xander said. "If we're going to find dirt on the guy, it'll be inside."

Dad shook his head. "I want to know who he sees. If he's planning another attack on us, he'll talk to people. We need to know who. Who can we trust, who we can't."

"*You* follow him," Xander said. "Dae and I will stay here."

Dad said, "I don't think—"

"Dad," Xander said, "we may never have this chance again. We're actually getting the upper hand for a change. We have so many things to do, we're going to have to split up sometime."

Dad considered it. He turned to David. "Dae?"

He raised his eyebrows. "You should have seen us get away from the berserkers this morning."

"The *what?*" Dad held up his hand. "Tell me later." He pulled out his mobile phone and turned to Xander. "Got yours?"

"Right here," Xander said. He fished it out of his back pocket.

"I got a signal," Dad said.

"Me too."

Dad said, "I'll call you if he heads back this way. Otherwise, we'll coordinate a rendezvous after we see what's what."

"Got it," Xander said.

Dad stood. "Keys?"

"In it."

Dad took off, booking through the woods like a deer.

David reopened a space in the bushes. "Think it's empty?" he said.

"No other cars."

"That doesn't mean anything," he said. "Besides, what about the garage?"

"One way to find out," Xander said. He pushed through the bushes.

He was halfway across the yard when David emerged. "Xander!" David whispered. It wasn't the stealthy approach he had imagined.

Xander strode across the concrete pad in front of the garage and went around to the other side. David reached the corner just as Xander was pulling his face from a closed window.

"There's an old Jeep in the garage," Xander said. "But it's up on blocks, and the engine is hanging from a chain." He hurried around David, cut across the front of the house, and jumped onto the front stoop.

Before David could stop him, Xander pounded on the door. David backed away. He scanned the perimeter of the clearing: so dark and dense, someone could be watching them and they'd never know.

Xander pounded again. He tried the knob. "Locked," he said. "Come on." He hopped down and stopped in front of the bay window. He cupped his hands around his face and looked in.

A part of David expected Xander to reel back in horror, saying something like, *Bodies! Bodies everywhere! Run!*

"What is it?" David said quickly: *Whatizit?*

"A living room," Xander said. He took a step back to examine the glass. "These don't open." He studied David for a moment. "You with me?"

David walked toward him. "All the way."

"Good. Let's try around back."

David watched him slip around the corner. *I can do this,* he thought, swallowing hard. He headed for the corner, his mind crowded with a thousand possible scenarios, all of them bad. At least he didn't hear Xander screaming—yet.

forty-seven

Thursday, 5:30 p.m.

Upon hitting the main road, Taksidian turned toward town.

Ed King hung back as much as he dared. A half mile later, he almost lost the Mercedes. He didn't see it turn off, but he noticed a dirt road coming up on the right. He passed it slowly and caught a glimpse of two red orbs glowing in the trees. Brake lights. He pulled over, let a car pass, then reversed to the road.

This one wasn't as treacherous as the ruts leading to Taksidian's house. *Probably a hunter's road,* he thought. It was on the other side of the main road from the house and obviously more heavily traveled. It brought him higher and higher into the hills, sometimes steeply, sometimes gradually, but always up.

He had not seen another sign of the Mercedes since the turnoff, but he'd passed no other roads. It had to be up ahead. He wasn't sure what he'd do if it came roaring back toward him. Turn his head, pretend to be someone else, maybe; hope Taksidian didn't stop to question him.

He crested another rise and stopped. The road leveled off here for a stretch. It cut through a valley, formed by woodsy hills on both sides. A few hundred yards farther on, the Mercedes was parked in the weeds on the side of the road. Its windows were too dark to see if Taksidian sat behind the wheel. No movement. No brake lights.

Mr. King killed the Bug's engine and poked his head out the window: no music.

He depressed the clutch and let the car roll back down the hill. He coasted onto the shoulder and got out. He didn't see any way to hide it this time. He only hoped he could leave before Taksidian. At least it was a car the man wouldn't recognize as belonging to the Kings. Taksidian couldn't get any nastier, but if he knew they were investigating him, he could make their task much more difficult.

He stayed close to the tree line as he approached the sedan. Twenty yards behind it, he crouched and watched. When nothing drew his attention, he moved in. The passenger's window was down. No one in the front seat. He crossed the weedy shoulder and peered in. Empty.

He examined the woods. It wasn't as dark or dense as Taksidian's property; this was more like the woods around the Kings' house.

Noises reached him. Voices drifting in the still air. They were faint, but he thought they were coming from the hill on the same side of the road as the Mercedes. He went among the trees and spotted a trail. It wound through the trees, up the hill.

He spent a full minute staring into the woods in all directions. Seeing no one staring back, he stepped onto the trail and began following it.

CHAPTER

forty-eight

THURSDAY, 5:45 P.M.

"Got it!" Xander said.

He was standing on a trash can to reach a window set into
the back of the house. They had tried all the ones they could
reach without assistance, plus a sliding glass door. The ground
at the back corner of the house, opposite the garage, sloped to
a creek. And wouldn't you know, it would be the window in
that corner, the hardest one to reach, that would be unlocked.

"Doesn't it open wider?" David said.

Xander grunted. "That's it."

"Can you fit? I could try."

"I'll do it."

"What's inside?" David said.

"Give me a minute." Xander pulled himself onto the sill. He twisted sideways and slipped in. His hips and butt wedged in the opening, but he wiggled them through. He stuck his head out. "It's a bedroom." He leaned out sideways and extended his hands toward David.

David crawled onto the trash can. It wobbled under his knees, then his feet. He had kept it steady for Xander, but without anyone holding it for him, it became another obstacle to overcome. It tilted, almost fell, then came back under his weight. He grabbed Xander's hands, and the can toppled out from under him. It tumbled down to the creek. Xander hoisted him inside.

When David spilled off the windowsill to the carpeted floor, Xander said, "You've been packing on the pounds, man."

"I doubt it," David said. "All the stuff we've been doing? I'm ready for the Olympics." He stood and looked around. The room wasn't so much dark as it was gloomy. As starkly furnished as a motel room: bed, nightstand, dresser, lamp.

"Nothing," David said. "Like the kitchen and living room." He had looked through the sliding glass doors into those areas. They were as plain as a slice of white bread. Some magazines on a coffee table, a glass on a table—they were the only things suggesting that someone lived here.

Xander stepped out into a hallway. David was right on him. He resisted the temptation to grab hold of his brother's shirt. The ordinariness of the place didn't fool him. This was Taksidian's lair. There was nothing ordinary about the man; he was certain that under its humdrum appearance, there was something very *un*ordinary about this house.

"Bingo," Xander said.

Here we go.

His brother was standing in the doorway of another room. David pushed past him and entered the room.

A countertop ran the length of one wall. On it, two computer monitors displayed screensavers: On one, a crest of some kind, depicting an eagle with the tail of a snake. The tail formed a circle around the bird. On the other was a painting. An ancient battle. A warrior stood atop a hill, slashing his sword down at combatants rising to fight him. David realized that the mound on which the warrior stood wasn't earth, but corpses.

Scraps of paper and computer printouts littered the rest of the countertop.

Two filing cabinets were so stuffed with documents, none of their drawers could close. The walls were plastered with maps, diagrams, photocopies of the pages of books, newspaper articles, photographs . . . every sort of printed matter David could imagine.

The wall on David's right seemed dedicated to war. A world map was marked with battles throughout time: Tanga (AD 1914); Avarayr (AD 451); Kohima (AD 1944); Jerusalem (AD 70); Hastings (AD 1066); San Jacinto (AD 1836); Troy (1193–83 BC) . . . hundreds of them. Around the map, Taksidian had taped articles about weapons, strategies, commanders: the discovery of gunpowder in ninth-century China; the first atomic bomb, called "Little Boy," detonated on Hiroshima in 1945 . . . Napoleon, Genghis Khan, Alexander the Great. Lines in different-colored ink connected the battles to each other and to the articles.

"It's like what we're doing in the MCC," David said. "He's mapping history, but only wars."

"Not *only* wars," Xander said. He was staring at another wall.

As David took it in, his stomach cramped tighter and tighter.

The wall was covered from floor to ceiling with pictures, diagrams, notes—all of them related to the Kings and their house.

CHAPTER

forty-nine

THURSDAY, 5:57 P.M.

Ed King reached a sloping meadow. He put his hands on his knees and breathed. He had stopped hearing the voices about five minutes ago, and the trail didn't seem to lead anywhere. He stretched his back and looked around. A picturesque hillside, but nothing more. No cabins, no fire pits, no people . . . no Taksidian.

Where are you? he thought. *What is this all about?*

Then he heard it: the slamming of a car door—faint in the distance.

The dull hum of an engine, revving, revving.

Music—that quick-rhythm weird stuff from Taksidian's car.

No, no!

He ran. Before reaching the woods, he saw the black Mercedes on the road. It crested the hill over which he had parked. Its hulking body rose up and slammed down, it had taken the hill so fast. Then it disappeared.

He heard it sliding to a stop. The top of its roof reappeared, barely visible on the other side of the hill. A cloud of yellow dust caught up with it and engulfed it. When it cleared, Taksidian was standing on the road, gazing at him.

He stumbled down farther and stopped. "Taksidian!" he yelled.

The man's head and shoulders lowered below the level of the hill, as though he had crouched down.

"Taksidian!"

A dozen seconds later, the car door slammed again, and the roof glided out of view. A wall of dust rose in its place.

Mr. King tore down the hill.

How'd you do it? he thought. *How did you return to the car without my seeing you?*

He had to have known he was being followed. No other way.

How long before Taksidian reached his house? Ten minutes. Less—a lot less if he hauled. And he was hauling!

Running, in the trees now, he pulled the mobile phone out of his pocket. He flipped it open with his thumb. His foot snagged on a tree root, and he fell. He flipped and slipped, crashed into a tree. The phone was not in his hand. He scampered back up. There: banked up on a rock.

Don't be broken! Don't be!

He picked it up. It appeared to be fine. Except for the words flashing on the screen: *No service.*

No!

He pushed Xander's speed-dial number anyway. When he held the phone to his ear, it was as silent as a dead man.

He ran. Under branches, over crevasses, through thickets of leaves, twigs, thorns.

He crashed out of the trees and tumbled into the weeds. He scrambled up, stumbled onto the road. The phone was still out of range. He took off for the hill and the Bug.

Taksidian had a couple minutes' head start on him. But he only needed to get to where his phone worked. Then he could call, tell Xander and David to get away from the house before Taksidian arrived.

He ran to the hill, down to the Bug.

He stopped so fast, his feet slid out from under him. The two tires on the driver's side of the car were flat. Long, ragged gouges in their sidewalls showed where Taksidian had slashed them.

Mr. King got to his feet. Checked the phone: no service. He pulled open the VW's door, climbed in, and started the engine.

I don't care about the tires, he thought. *If it'll roll with them flat, it'll have to be good enough.*

But he wasn't sure it *would* roll. He put the car in gear, popped the clutch, and punched the gas. The engine roared. The car lurched forward, bounding up and down as though he'd driven over boulders.

He cranked the wheel, and the Bug's front end swung around in the road.

Go! Go! Go! he cheered it on, though the desperation cramping his mind was anything but cheery.

The shredded tires thumped, throwing him up, sideways, around, each time. *Thump . . . thump . . . thump.*

The feeling of driving over boulders never changed. He bounced in his seat. The steering wheel jerked one way, then the other, but somehow he kept the car moving in a somewhat straight direction. He thought that if his course were drawn on a piece of paper, it would look like the scrabblings of a shaky-handed old man.

But he was moving . . . and building speed: *thump-thump-thump-thump-thump.*

Every fifteen or twenty *thumps,* he squinted at the phone. No bars, no service.

Come on! Come on!

He shifted, pressed his foot harder against the gas pedal.

The bug slid around on the dirt road as though on ice.

Mr. King's head hit the ceiling. His shoulder slammed against the door. Still, he willed the car to go faster.

I'm coming, boys, he thought, praying that somehow his words would reach his sons. *Hide . . . fight . . . do whatever you have to do! I'm coming!*

CHAPTER

fifty

THURSDAY, 6:14 P.M.

"Take a picture," David said.

Xander pulled out his phone, stepped back from the wall, and snapped a shot. The flash made each piece of paper appear to jump out at David: photographs of the Kings coming out of the house, David sitting in class, Dad climbing into the 4Runner, Toria opening the oven—seemingly taken from outside the kitchen window; diagrams of each floor of the house, including the third. In each of the ante-chambers, Taksidian had scribbled words in a language David didn't know. He didn't even recognize the letters.

Xander snapped another picture.

The photo that jumped out at David was of Dad pumping gas into the 4Runner. The heads of David, Xander, and Toria were blurry shadows behind the windows. It was the same gas station where they had watched Taksidian talk to the mechanic earlier today.

A memory hit David's brain like a blast of liquid nitrogen, freezing it. He grabbed Xander's arm.

"He knows!" David said. "Taksidian knows we're here. He knows we followed him."

"David, no! He can't. How do you—"

"The stops he made on the way to his house! The grocery store, the fast-food place, the gas station. Xander, they're the exact places I said he would go when you wanted to follow him. In the exact same order. Remember, I said, 'a hundred nothing things at a hundred nothing places.'"

"But how—"

"Who cares *how*? He knew all along. He was playing with us. He was showing us he knew. I *thought* something was weird, but I didn't get it!" He made a fist and wanted to punch himself.

Xander looked down at the phone. He tapped a button.

"What are you doing?" David said. "We have to get out of here! Now!"

"Calling Dad," Xander said. "He'd have called us if—"

Music came out of the tiny speaker. Xander glared at the phone. His forehead wrinkled like an old man's. "What—?"

"That's the music Taksidian was listening to in his car," David said.

Xander turned on the speaker function. The weird chanting filled the room, then stopped.

"It's called an infinity transmitter," Taksidian said, his voice deep and gravelly. "It allows me to turn on the microphone of any phone for which I have the number. No ringing, just an open connection. So I can listen to everything said within earshot of your phone. Shouldn't bring phones to school, you know." He laughed a hearty laugh that echoed.

Xander snapped the phone shut, but the booming laughter continued.

An engine growled outside, rising in volume. David ran to the window. Taksidian's Mercedes bounced out of the rutted drive into the front yard. It slid to a stop.

"He's here!" David said.

"Let's go!" Xander ran into the hallway, turned into the living room.

Now David did grab his brother's shirt. He pointed. "The sliding glass door!"

They ran to it, tugged, tugged. Xander flipped a small lever on the handle. It still didn't budge.

"It's barred," David said. He had his hands on a metal rod

that ran from the rear of the door to the frame. "It must be locked too. Or welded."

They spun around.

Across the living room, the front door's dead bolt rattled.

"Go!" Xander said. He shoved David toward another short hallway on the opposite side of the living room from Taksidian's office.

"No," David said. "The window!" He ran toward the bedroom. The bolt snapped open, and David realized he didn't have time. Taksidian would grab his legs as he slithered out. He knew panic was jumbling his thoughts, making him confused, but there was no reining them in now.

He spun around. Xander, thinking David was half out the window by now, darted into a room and slammed the door.

David shot to the nearest door in sight: a narrow pantry off the kitchen. He yanked open the door, stepped inside, and pulled it shut.

The darkness was complete, as though a shroud had dropped over him. Wind swirled up from the floor. He felt the walls closing in on him. The floor under him shifted.

He knew this feeling! The linen closet portal did this. But . . . but . . . *here?* How?

Wait!

He grabbed for the door handle. It was gone.

His fingers slid along cold, wet rock.

CHAPTER

fifty-one

THURSDAY, 6:18 P.M.

Xander pressed his back to the door. He squeezed his eyes
tight. His lungs pumped in air, pushed it out. His heart was
a fist pounding into his throat.

*Please, Lord, let David get away. Let him be outside and running away
right now.*

Something banged against a side wall. *The front door,* he
thought.

He opened his eyes. No light at all. He considered where he

was in the house. To the right of the front door, if you were looking at the house. He was in the room with the bricked-up window.

He reached behind him, felt the door handle. A button in the center. He depressed it. A simple lock, but something.

The room hummed. Either a fan was on or there was some serious ventilation in the place.

He had to find a weapon. Scissors, a piece of wood, anything. He raised his hand to the wall, searching for the light switch.

What is that smell? he thought. Sour, rotten.

His fingers found the switch. He flipped it up.

The walls were painted black; the ceilings and wooden floor, bright red. Hanging on the wall where the window used to be was a costume consisting of a woven shirt and a skirt made of strips of leather, each tipped with a metal triangle. Over the shirt's sleeves were mounted iron armguards, scarred by the blades they'd parried. A short, black leather sheath clung to the wall near the top of the skirt. The knife or dagger belonging to the sheath was missing. Rips and cuts disfigured the shirt; maroon stains bordered and spread out from each rent.

The other walls contained similar artifacts: a sword, a shield, spears, a bow and arrows, a tattered banner, beads, jewelry, metal and wooden face masks. Small lights set into the ceiling shone on the items, museumlike.

Despite the abundance of weaponry, Xander felt no joy, no

relief. Only terror. For his eyes had settled on an object in the center of the room. It was lighted from all sides, as fine statues are. Rising from a short pedestal, the sculpture was somewhat circular, like a pillar. But it was rough, with parts jutting out.

Parts, Xander thought. *Body parts!*

Arms, legs, ears, fingers—all cobbled together to create a monstrous monument to death. The stench; the unmistakable decay that had laid claim to various limbs; the evidence of tissue, muscle, bone within each visible stub: Xander knew without doubt that this was no fabrication; each piece had once belonged to a living human.

Beside the horrific pillar was a stainless steel table on wheels, like the ones on medical shows. A scalpel, paintbrush, and bottles rested on it. And something else.

Not wanting to know, needing to know, he stepped closer. Before he realized it, he was leaning over the object on the table.

It was a finger. White as Carrara marble. The flesh had shriveled, leaving what amounted to bones and knuckles encased in wrinkled skin. The fingernail gleamed.

Xander knew it was Jesse's.

The door behind him banged open.

Xander spun. He reversed away from the figure stepping in: Taksidian, a smile on his face, a knife in his hand.

Xander's heels hit the pedestal.

He toppled backward into the pillar.

CHAPTER

fifty-two

Darkness. David might as well have been blind.

He felt the walls around him. They were cold and wet. And he could touch them on all sides. Not much larger than a casket standing on end. Gravel crunched under his sneakered feet. It shifted easily, making it difficult to stand.

The air was humid. He smelled nothing but his own sweat.

Where am I? How could Taksidian's house have a portal? This isn't possible! This isn't happening!

David struck the wall in front of him. His fist cracked into it with a thud. No give. No echo of sound on the other side either.

He patted the walls. He didn't find a door handle or hinges or cracks. He reached up. There seemed to be no top. A foot over his head, a stone or brick protruded a few inches from the surrounding surface. He pushed it, pulled it, tried to make it wiggle. It was solid.

His fingertips touched a loose item on top of the protruding stone. He picked it up and shook it. He knew the rattling it made. It was a box of wooden matches.

Yes!

He gently pushed the inner tray out from its cardboard sleeve. He withdrew a stick, identified the match tip, and struck it against the sleeve's side. It sparked. He tried again. The matched flared, settled into a flame.

The walls were as he had imagined: gray squares—blocks, probably—ten inches to a side. They appeared to be resting against one another with no mortar between them. They glistened with moisture, but he couldn't see where the water was coming from. Scratches ran vertically in the center of each wall, from head height to chest.

The flame touched his thumb and fingertip. He dropped the match and licked his burned skin. He lit another.

He looked up to the protruding stone. It was nothing more, just a workman's error, it seemed. High above, the ceiling appeared to be a single slab of granite. Dangling from it by something he couldn't see was a lantern.

Another *yes!*

He stretched, tiptoed, but his fingers were still a hand's length from the bottom of the lantern. He shook out the match before it could bite again. Struck another.

He turned and confirmed that the walls were unbroken by doors or openings of any kind. The gravel shifted. He fell into a wall, straightened. He squinted into the darkness below. The light faded before reaching the floor. He bent down.

A skull's eyeless sockets stared up at him. He screamed and dropped the match. Before it flickered out, he saw that the entire floor was covered not with gravel, but with bones. Leg bones. Arm bones. He caught a glimpse of a rib cage and a spine. Most of the ones still whole enough to recognize lay around the outer edge. The rest had been ground and broken into dust and small fragments.

Crushed by how many feet? he thought. How many people had been trapped here? How many people had contributed their own bones to the floor?

He pounded on the wall. "Help! Help me, please! Xander!"

His eyes stung. He wiped at them, smearing tears.

"Help!" he yelled. "Can anyone hear me?"

He fell back against a wall, lifted his face, and screamed.

NOT THE END . . .

WITH SPECIAL THANKS TO . . .

The first "Dream the Scene" winners: JOSHUA RUARK, who suggested the King kids should walk through a portal into ninth-century England, during the Viking raid on Alfred the Great's castle. There, they face a bloodthirsty berserker. And KATIE O'DELL, who thought the Kings should suddenly find themselves on the deck of the Titanic, as it's sinking. Wonderful ideas! I hope you like how they played out in the story.

SLADE PEARCE, for *being* David: you rock!

NICHOLAS and LUKE FALLENTINE (again): you guys are great

BEN and MATTHEW FORD, insightful readers and my new friends

ALEC OBERNDORFER, ALIX CHANDLER, MADDIE WILLIAMS, sharp-eyed and quick-minded early readers

ANTHONY, my son and most fervent fan

JOEL GOTLER, my wonderful agent

The rest of my family, for letting me be a kid again

LB NORTON, JUDY GITENSTEIN, and AMANDA BOSTIC, editors extraordinaire

The terrific team at Nelson: ALLEN, JOCELYN, JENNIFER, KATIE, MARK, LISA, BECKY . . .

And my readers, for letting the King family live!

READING GROUP GUIDE

1. Keal talks about doing what's right. How do we distinguish right from wrong? Have you ever done something you thought was right, only to find out later it was the wrong thing to do? What did you do about it?

2. If you could go back in time and change something in the past, what would it be? If you could meet anyone from history, who would it be? Why? What do you think you'd learn or gain from the experience?

3. The Kings have faced all sorts of dangers and endured all kinds of injuries, yet they keep pressing on—all for the sake of rescuing Mom. Have you ever wanted something so badly, you've continued going for it, even when it seemed everything was against your getting it? From where did you find the strength to carry on? What was the outcome? Have you ever given up and then later wished you hadn't?

4. To stay in the house and find Mom, the Kings are learning to be tough and figure things out. Can you see ways in which each of the family members has changed since coming to Pinedale? In what ways? What situation have you gone through that changed you, how you think of things, handle things?

5. Clayton is a typical bully: he made fun of David in class, threatened to beat him up, and chased him through locker 119 into the house. David finally got the upper hand, scaring Clayton and taking a picture of him crying. But in *Timescape*, David tries to make amends. Why do you think he tried to make peace with Clayton? Have you ever been picked on by a bully? What happened? What do you think is the best way to handle bullies? Have you ever been a bully yourself? How did it make you feel?

6. David and Xander often gear themselves up for action by saying "Strong and courageous!" This is an exhortation used many times in the Bible, such as I Chronicles 22:13: *Be strong and courageous. Do not be afraid or discouraged.* What is your favorite Bible verse? Why? Do you have any saying you tell yourself when you have to do something brave or difficult?

7. Xander wants to press on despite being exhausted. Do you agree with Keal's argument that sleep isn't a break from going after a goal—it is an essential *part* of achieving that goal? When was the last time you were forced to sleep even though a strong desire to do something made you not want to?

8. What do you think Taksidian is doing that caused the destruction of Los Angeles—and presumably the rest of the world? What can the Kings do to prevent it? The Kings finally go on the offensive to protect themselves from Taksidian. Why do you think Dad went along with Xander's plan to tail Taksidian? Do you agree with the saying "The best defense is a strong offense"? What does that mean to you? Give an example of a time when you went on the offensive to defend yourself.

9. Which one of the "worlds" the Kings have visited so far is your favorite? Why?

GO **DEEPER**

INTO

THE **WORLD** OF

the
dreamhouse kings

ROBERTLIPARULO.COM/BLOG

THE ADVENTURE
CONTINUES WITH

BOOK 5 IN THE DREAMHOUSE KINGS SERIES